I0546076

RESCUES

THE HITMAN

--- PULLING THREADS ---

Book Eight

SHERYLL O'BRIEN

This is a work of fiction. All characters in this book are the product of an overactive imagination. Any businesses, organizations, places, events, and incidents are used fictionally. Any resemblance to a real person, living or dead, is a tremendous coincidence.

Copyright © 2020 by Sheryll O'Brien
All rights reserved

ISBN 978-1-939351-17-3

WOODWIND PRESS

Printed in United States of America

Mom,

I still chuckle at your comment ---
"Good Lord,
Malcolm and Gretchen
Sure do love the shower!"

ACKNOWLEDGMENT

To all of the Women out there who are
Fierce when they have to be – and
Vulnerable when they want to be.

A heartfelt thank you to my team:

Andria Flores ~ Editor extraordinaire.
Nancy Pendleton ~ Goddess of the publishing world.
Jessica Champion ~ Web designer and manager.
25 Hours Consulting
Daryl Bruinsma ~ Cover Design & Animation.

Testimonials

"One book will set the hook!" ~ Nancy Pendleton

"This avid reader predicts that Sheryll O'Brien will become your favorite author. She's mine." ~ Ruth S. Bodreau

"The characters draw you in immediately. You will worry, laugh, hope, and love right along with them." ~ Donna Eaton

"There is nothing sweeter than a Sunday morning coffee, a blanket, overcast skies, and a *Pulling Threads* novel." ~ Andria Flores

"Everything you'd want in a good book. Humor, romance, suspense and great characters! It even takes place by the ocean! Loved it." ~ Helena Green

"I could write a book about the wonderfulness of it all." ~ Faith Lavallee

"Hunks, humor, and heartache! What more could you ask for?" ~ Marjorie McCarthy

"*Bullet Bungalow* is a page turning family saga and then *Netti Barn* and *Cutters Cove* come along and add a whole lot of trauma to the drama." ~ Jessica O'Brien

"The most promising new author I've encountered in my publishing career!" ~ Jim P. - Woodwind Press

--- Pulling Threads ---

Bullet Bungalow
Netti Barn
Cutters Cove
They Run
They Hide
They Choose

PENOBSCOT BAY
A Rocco Fiancetti Incorporated Investigation

Reasons
Rescues

Coming soon…

Resolutions
Torment
Tango
Tests
Resolve
Revenge
Rebound

--- Twisted Threads ---

Coming soon…

Her Scream
Stay Safe

From paradise to prison.

U.S. Bureau of Prisons inmate BOP-PA-555925 is locked in a cell and gripped by a nightmare…

"You are American?" he asked the naturally pretty, strawberry-blonde woman sitting across from him on the near-empty, first-class flight heading to Belize.

"Born in Paris, raised in America, and until very recently living again in Paris, and you?"

"Sort of," he said with a wide smile.

"A man of mystery," she said with a toss of her soft shoulder-length ringlets.

He liked the way her slightly upturned, freckled nose crinkled when she smiled wide. He particularly liked her light, easy way. "Are you vacationing in Belize?"

"Yes, and you?"

"Sort of," he said with a wide smile.

"The mystery continues," she chuckled.

"The Mayan ruins, is that your fascination with Belize?" he asked.

"Yes, of course, but the Belize Barrier Reef is my true fascination. I've heard the watering of Belize is like no other."

"Watering?"

Her laugh was free, infectious. "Snorkeling, scuba diving, rafting, kayaking, that sort of thing."

"A woman of watering? Never would have guessed it," he smiled.

She raised her glass of white wine in mock toast. "Guess I'm a woman of mystery, too," she laughed—a wonderful laugh.

~

"Love the treehouse," he said as he started toward the outside staircase. He stopped at the landing, waiting for his companion to head up. She was nowhere in sight.

"Over here, Manuel."

He turned toward her call and watched as she made her way up a rope ladder that was affixed to a nearby tree, as she pressed her back tight against the trunk, and as she pushed into a standing position. She unfurled a length of rope hooked to the side, grabbed it high, wrapped the ends tightly around her hands, and pushed off, the momentum swinging her and bringing her to the building he thought they'd be entering in a more ordinary fashion. He smiled w.i.d.e. "I see watering isn't your only form of physical fitness."

"Get your ass up here, and I'll show you what else I can do."

~

Dominique was startled when Manuel dropped onto the first-class seat next to her. "What are you doing? I thought you left—because you needed to get back for your job?"

"I said I had something to do for work. I didn't say I was leaving Belize."

She furrowed her brow and tilted her head. "But you took your things."

"In case I couldn't get back before *you* left." He took hold of her hand and gave it a gentle squeeze. "I took care of what needed to be done and went back to the treehouse at Hamanasi. You were gone. I thought you were staying another few days, maybe another week."

The sun-kissed cheeks of the beautiful freckle-faced woman reddened and held the heat of the moment. "I... I..." she sighed and stared out the plane's window. "A month's vacation was enough. It's time to move on," she said over her shoulder.

Manuel stood, reached into his pocket, and sat back down. Dominique turned and watched his movements—she wished she hadn't when he showed her the pregnancy test he found discarded back at Hamanasi. "I think we have things to discuss, Dominique."

Surprise then upset flashed and settled on her face. "You shouldn't..."

"No, Dominique, you shouldn't. No, Dominique, you shouldn't. No, Dominique, you shouldn't."

"No!"

Rescues

LewPen

Attorney, Gretchen Mitchell, daughter of famed attorney, Granger Mitchell, sits in a meeting room at Lewisburg Penitentiary awaiting the arrival of inmate BOP-PA-555925, also known as Dominique Brettenvue. Today marks Gretchen's third visit to the female wing of LewPen and it looks as though she is going to leave without seeing the prisoner. Again. That circumstance is noteworthy. Prisoners, particularly those serving life sentences in solitary confinement, are generally eager to leave their cells and spend time with another human being, even if that human being is a lawyer. And yet, Gretchen Mitchell sits alone. Again. Sort of.

Inside the meeting room with her and standing sentry at the locked meeting room door is a correctional officer — the same CO who has been in attendance for all three non-meetings. Neither of the two individuals within those tight quarters has said Word One during any of their time together, and yet their body language has spoken **volumes**.

Things are about to change.

The first thing people notice about the 32-year-old Harvard Law graduate is that she is white — in every way imaginable. Her skin is pearly-white, her hair is platinum-blonde, her perfectly straight teeth shine bright through a perfectly wide smile, and though she is a lawyer, the lies she tells are generally of the white variety. As the minutes of her half-hour visit tick past without BOP-PA-555925 joining her, the woman who is getting noticed by the prison guard seeks a bit more attention. She stretches her long, toned legs, and taps her perfectly manicured fingers on the envelope that sits on a table next to her. She enjoys the man's attention as his eyes travel the length of her, all 5'11" of it. She imagines he is wondering what state her pussy is in; for the record, it's uncovered by hair and by panties. Gretchen tosses her stick straight, shoulder length, platinum hair away from her face and waits for it to settle back in place before sending him a smile.

The big, bald, beautiful MAN returns the smile as he watches the sleek hair show, and when it stops moving, his eyes lock onto her brilliant blues. He shifts his weight between his feet – his movement drawing her eyes down the length of him, stopping at the outline of his erection. She smiles, fans her hand in front of her face to lift a little air, reaches down and undoes the top two buttons of her blouse then separates the neckline. She shifts in her seat spreading her bare legs just enough, and yet not nearly enough.

The guard groans low, just as a very loud buzzer overhead interrupts their sex play.

Gretchen gets up and struts to the guard. She hands him the envelope she's brought with her, "Would you put this into the appropriate channels for prisoner BOP-PA-555925?" She moves past the MAN to stand at the door just as he reaches past her to unlock it. His hand grazes one of her erect nipples, hers grazes his jutting wood.

She moans.

He groans.

"Guess the trip wasn't a waste of time, after all," she eyes the guard's name tag, "Correctional Officer, Price."

"Agreed, Attorney Mitchell."

Gretchen exits the room ahead of the guard, then follows quietly behind him to the security clearance area. Two things about that: Gretchen is rarely quiet and she is uninclined to follow a man – any man. As she hasn't a choice in the matter, she makes good use of her time, "Edgy yet graceful—like a big cat on the prowl—like a panther."

CO Price turns at her mumble, "Did you say something, Attorney Mitchell?"

"I don't think so." Eager to put this unsuccessful business errand behind her, she completes a visitor request form for the following week, a visit she suspects will not happen, takes her things from the desk guard, and with a wink and a smile for CO Price she walks out of prison. She removes her suit jacket on her way through the parking lot, lifts her face to the late-morning sun, gives her platinum hair a swing, and slides into her Diamond White Mercedes AMG GT R roadster, making sure to give another pussy peek to the CO who's watching from inside. Though there's really no need, she drives past the door she just exited, offers a bright smile, and swing of her hair to the MAN, shifts her ride and roars from the parking lot. "Damn, he's hot."

Gretchen opens the car's top then opens Diamond White on the highway. She rebuttons her blouse, throws on a pair of shades to cut the rising bright sun, cranks Kenny Chesney's *Get Along,* and begins her two-and-a-half-hour trip back to Philly. She takes note that everything she does on these weekly trips is becoming routine. Norah Jones on the drive in, Kenny Chesney on the drive home, and thoughts of the correctional officer when she slips into bed at night.

Halfway back to her office, the young lawyer's thoughts start banging and clanging, and words begin tripping from her lips, "Yes, sir, I know this is a disappointment. Yes, I know the Brettenvues expect results. The situation is this, Dominique simply refuses to meet with me.

There isn't much I can do to rectify that whilst under guard in a lawyer's meeting room." Gretchen hates disappointing her boss almost as much as she hates disappointing her father. In this case, they are one and the same. She tries out another tactic. "We know why Dominique refuses to meet with the Brettenvues – perhaps we shouldn't be representing these vile people. They fucked up colossally with their own daughter, do we really want to help them get another baby?" Gretchen. Laughs. Out. Loud. "I could NEVER say those words to Granger Mitchell. Even though they should be said."

Solitary Confinement

Dominique Brettenvue sits crossed-legged on her one-inch rubber mattress on her concrete slab bed rocking gently back and forth. She has her hands wrapped under and around her baby belly, the words of a French lullaby filling the space between mother and unborn child. "Ah Mon beau château..."

The expectant prisoner angsts that the days she has with her baby are coming to a close. Once her daughter is born, she will be taken and placed in the custody of the Commonwealth of Pennsylvania without Dominique having ever laid eyes on her. The angry woman pulls a noisy breath. "I wish we were still at Big Sandy," she gently rubs her baby bump, "if you were born in Kentucky, my sweet one, you could grow up in the Bluegrass State with all the pretty horses." She evil eyes the yellow envelopes set at the foot of her slab. "Now that I'm back in Pennsylvania you'll have to live in the same hellish state as the people who adopted me, raised me, and ruined me."

The prisoner gathers the stack of envelopes, "Opened," she sneers. "Someone in this hellhole knows what's in these." She runs her finger over the raised navy embossed Mitchell and Morgan, Attorneys at Law, return address label in the left-hand corner before putting each envelope into one of two piles. "These four envelopes were sent to Mommy when she was at Big Sandy in Kentucky, and these three have been hand-delivered to Mommy, here. Every week, a handsome correctional officer delivers an envelope and a visitation request form on behalf of an attorney who works for Mitchell and Morgan." Dominique gathers the envelopes together and tosses them onto the floor, "Why the hell would I meet with an attorney who works for Mitchell and Morgan, especially if that lawyer is Gretchen Mitchell?" she scoffs, then begins cooing to her baby again, "Mommy shouldn't have cussed, sweet little one."

The pregnant woman unfolds her crossed legs, inches herself to the edge of the slab, puts her feet onto the floor and her hand on her baby

bulge and whispers, "Time for Mommy to take her little one for a walk. Along the way, mon cheri, I'll tell you all about your papa."

Time is ticking.

Benton Brettenvue, Founder and CEO of The Brettenvue Group, pours himself a stiff drink. He is on his third three fingers of whiskey and is quickly closing in on three sheets to the wind. It is a familiar place of late for the man who is taking incoming from all sides. For years, Benton was cock of the walk in the Keystone State, and The Brettenvue Group was the gold-standard for lobbying firms across the country. Today, the man teeters at the precipice of prison, and his namesake company teeters at the precipice of ruin. A few questionable actions with a notorious criminal enterprise led to inquiries, which led to investigations, which led to threats of arrest, which led nowhere. **So far**. The man who had it all – but who wanted more – knows that the next time the Feds come knocking on his door he will be going to jail.

The near drunk man slams his hand onto the ringing phone that dares disturb his bender. He grabs the receiver, accidently cracking it against his cheek. "Dammit! Who is this?"

"For the time being it's your attorney," Granger Mitchell answers.

"You're about to tell me that the felon refused to see the lawyer," Benton slurs.

"I am."

"Time is ticking, Granger. Celia and I want that baby. How are you going to make that happen?"

"Pull yourself together, Benton. We have a plan in place and we are executing that plan one step at a time. We needed Dominique out of Kentucky and in Pennsylvania — she's in Pennsylvania. When she gives birth, the baby will be placed with the Commonwealth's department of Child Protective Services. We will ask that the court grant custody of the baby to its maternal grandparents. You and Celia rub elbows with the people who make those kinds of decisions, so dry yourself out and be patient." Granger Mitchell hangs up.

Benton slams down the phone, picks up his tumbler and smashes it against the far wall of his office. He tries to get up, but is seemingly weighted to his chair. He starts an angry recitation of the attorney's words, "Dry yourself out and be patient. Dry yourself out and be patient. Dry yourself out and be patient." The thing is Benton doesn't want to dry out. When he is sober, or as close to sober as he allows himself to get, he starts thinking about Dominique. It is always the same memory that claws its way in…

He pulled onto the driveway, his car's headlights cutting across the family room windows finding a waiting pajama-clad grade schooler. Her muffled squeals could be heard coming from inside the status symbol house.

"Daddy's home. Daddy's home."

By the time he closed the front door behind him, she'd already run and tucked into her hiding place. "Where's Dominique?" he'd call out. "Did anyone see a little girl with strawberry-blonde ringlets and freckles on her nose, who stands about yay high?" he'd say as he pulled back a curtain here or looked behind a chair, there. "Dominique, you are getting very good at this hiding game," he'd say as he opened a closet door or peeked behind the cocktail bar. He'd let the game linger. Five minutes of Hide 'n Seek when she was five, six minutes when she was six, seven minutes when she was seven. That's when the fun and games stopped.

"That's when you turned the corner and started rubbing elbows with the wrong people," the spiraling man reminds himself, "a compromising decision here, a cross of the line there, then the deal with the Devil, the Peruvian Devil. And now, there's an expiration date on Dominique, and your own outstanding debts will be called in soon—very soon."

Benton pushes himself from his chair and crosses his office, the sound of shattered glass crunching beneath his shoes. He looks around his palatial digs, sneers at his success. When his bloodshot eyes fall upon a near bloodless reflection in a framed beveled glass mirror, he freezes at the sight. In a matter of a few months Benton Brettenvue has lost his once enviable youthful look. The gray in his hair is taking hold and multiplying tenfold each day. His eyes are crimson-rimmed and swollen. His pallor is sickly-jaundiced. His attire is unkept. His faculties are inert. The man scoffs at his mirrored appearance and continues his journey. He stumbles then rights himself as he reaches his office bar. The drunkard pours himself another round and raises his glass, "To Dominique," he slurs as he drains the amber liquid in one gulp. He smiles as the burn travels the length of him. The smile is short lived.

Celia Brettenvue, a completely retooled version of her younger model-worthy self, glides into her husband's office. "Granger called. He told me—**told me**—to get you sobered up. I told him I prefer you three sheets to the wind and wrapped in the sheets of your mistress."

"Shut up, Celia. Kindly remove yourself from my office," Benton's words a slur and delivered on a bit of spittle.

The bitter wife laughs at her wasted husband. "Granger said you need to dry yourself out and be patient. I told him you aren't capable of either of those things. He said you'd better get yourself in order or we won't get the baby when the time comes." Celia death-stares the man, a look of disgust trying to take hold of her perfectly nipped and tucked plastic face. "That baby better be in my arms at the end of June or else, Benton." On her way out of his office, she takes two bottles of single-malt whiskey from the office bar and closes the door behind her.

Benton Brettenvue, Founder and CEO of The Brettenvue Group, former cock of the walk, former associate of the Peruvian Devil, pulls open the bottom left-hand desk drawer and grabs a bottle of amber. He cracks the seal, takes a long pull, and passes out.

Mitchell and Morgan

Granger Mitchell, co-founding attorney of one of Philadelphia's most successful and highly regarded law firms sits at his massive mahogany desk having just made a call to a most distasteful client. He returns the handheld receiver to a rotary relic that he's been using since he opened his law firm thirty-five years ago. The phone has been part of the most important conversations of his life…

"Miss Delaney Rae Hamilton, this is Granger Mitchell calling for the pleasure of a date. … Mr. Hamilton, this is Granger Mitchell calling for the pleasure of Miss Delaney Rae's hand in marriage. … Darling, I will meet you promptly at the hospital. Yes, Yes. I am very excited about meeting our baby. …

Delaney Rae, extend your visit. Please do not get on that plane. ... Officers, are there any survivors?"

Gretchen sat motionless during the call between her father and the husband Brettenvue, and then during the one he had with the wife Brettenvue. She enjoyed the authoritative directive when he told the society doyenne to sober up her husband or be prepared to suffer a loss in court. What Gretchen did not discern during either conversation – what she has yet to discern – is what Granger Mitchell thinks of their clients. This surprises her. Having been raised by the single father since the age of one, she believes she knows the mind of the man who shared his life with her, and no other for the past three decades. The lawyer, the father, the man always set expectations of conduct for himself, and for his daughter. His professional, parental, and personal style in all things was purposeful; focused on leading by example, molding morals and setting ethics at every turn. That's why Gretchen finds the untoward association between Granger Mitchell and Benton Brettenvue most perplexing. Truth be told, that isn't the only thing Gretchen ponders when it comes to Granger Mitchell. The most significant of her considerations center around his free time, and what he does with it.

"...so work. That's it, Daddy. You've done nothing else whilst I've been at UPenn? Perhaps I should return to the Cottage, and give up life in the dorms..."

~

"...so work. That's it, Daddy. You've done nothing else whilst I've been traipsing Europe. Perhaps I should return Stateside..."

~

"...so work. That's it, Daddy. You've done nothing else whilst I've been at Harvard? Perhaps I should transfer to UPenn Law..."

Granger Mitchell closed himself off from much of the world the day his wife died. The now 65-year old man attends only a handful of black-tie charity events each year, does not socialize, and does not date. In fact, Gretchen hasn't ever seen her father so much as speak to a woman who isn't a business associate, or the wife of a colleague, let alone spend time with a member of the female persuasion. A matter that has caused Gretchen considerable thought over the years...

"Surely, the man amongst men must have dalliances," Gretchen suggested to the closet thing she had to a BFF, Gaby Fisk. The college athletes competed vigorously as they looped around and hurdled over tracks and things, but by the time they ended their freshman year at

UPenn, they were ardent supporters of one another's pursuits, and very good friends.

"I can't imagine a reason why your father would discuss such things with you, Gretchen."

"No. No. Of course you're right, Gaby. Granger Mitchell wouldn't discuss such matters with me, but I've never heard a single word about his personal life— from anyone." She shared that bit of trivia while she and Gaby were belly-up at O'Toole's Tavern in the village Mayo, in County Mayo, Ireland. "Daddy might not be the sharing type, but people love to gossip, and never has a word of gossip been said about Granger Mitchell."

The same cannot be said by Granger Mitchell – the man has heard rumors – many, many rumors about Gretchen's love life.

The senior partner clears his throat bringing his daydreaming daughter back to the here and now. He has had pen to paper since he ended his call with Celia Brettenvue and hands the navy embossed piece of personal stationery to Gretchen. The elder Mitchell never tells his daughter what he expects from her, he writes down what he needs or wants. That has been his way since Gretchen was old enough to read, and before that he wrote his notes and gave his lists to her nannies, without comment.

Gretchen reads the handwritten directive and turns astonished eyes to her father. "You want me to try to get a message to Dominique at the Federal penitentiary?"

"Yes," he stops to clear his throat, "I hear you have certain wiles with men that you may be willing to use."

Gretchen shifts uncomfortably in her seat. "Yes, well, outside a Federal penitentiary perhaps, but isn't this sort of thing frowned upon?"

"Yes, so don't screw it up." Granger Mitchell begins reading an email signaling the end of their meeting.

Peruvian Devil

Antonio Alvarez, an upper echelon leader of the recently decimated criminal organization known worldwide as The Realm, sits in a meeting room with his lawyer, Stuart Howard. Little was known about the nefarious global enterprise before it was disbanded – little is known now; with one notable exception — The Realm sought to control the intelligence gathering domain known as cyberland by kidnapping the #1, #2, and #3 world-ranked cyber huntresses, Joy Fiancetti, Annie Mahoney-Maxwell, and Hannah Leavy, respectively. Rocco Fiancetti Incorporated, known worldwide as RFI, is the international law enforcement team that broke The Realm, aided in part by Dominique Brettenvue, a wannabe Realm leader, and Baby Mama of Antonio Alvarez's demonic offspring.

After months of wrangling with governmental agencies across the globe, the United States gained custody of Alvarez and is holding him at the ADX Florence Supermax Penitentiary in Colorado. There is a mile-long list of countries that want to bring Antonio Alvarez to trial. The U.S. tops that list, so when the Feds got custody of The Realm leader, they put him where no one can get to him.

The crime lord should be spending his meeting with his lawyer focusing on his criminal case, but rather he is raging about two things: Dominique Brettenvue and RFI. Alvarez verbally lashes his lawyer from the confines of a concrete chair that rises from a concrete floor. The criminal's hands and feet are shackled, his body is chained to the slab at his waist, he can't move his hands more than six inches, and yet his lawyer fears for his life every time he steps into the meeting room with the Devil.

"Tell me about the puta," he says after ten minutes of fury—first in Spanish, then in Portuguese, then in English.

"Dominique is healthy. The baby is female." The lawyer holds his tongue until Alvarez responds.

He nods once. "Tell me about our plan to get mija after the puta delivers," Alvarez says calmly.

"Immediately after birth, the Commonwealth of Pennsylvania will take custody of the baby until an adoptive family is chosen. Your associates have someone inside CPS who has selected three families. They are being green lighted through the vetting process. The family that is selected will get the baby as an urgent foster care placement upon her birth, and will then petition to adopt the baby. That part of the process will take three months before a judge signs off on it. As soon as it is official, the adoptive parents will fly the baby to Peru and give her to your family."

Alvarez nods throughout the lawyer's speech, stops nodding when the lawyer shifts uncomfortably in his chair. "There's more," Alvarez hisses.

The lawyer nods before broaching the subject he fears will set off the Devil. "Now that Benton and Celia Brettenvue have Dominique in a penitentiary in Pennsylvania, the law firm representing them, or more specifically, Granger Mitchell, the senior partner in the firm, is pushing hard to get them custody of the baby. The court that will ultimately make the custody decision is on Brettenvue's home turf. The maternal grandparents may have a better chance of getting the baby than they did when Dominique was in Kentucky." The lawyer pauses before delivering more bad news. "The Brettenvues have been reaching out to Dominique through Mitchell and Morgan with weekly correspondence, and visits from an attorney with the law firm. According to information provided by your associates inside Lewisburg Penitentiary, Dominique hasn't read the correspondence or met with the attorney, yet."

"Who is the visiting attorney?"

"Gretchen Mitchell, Granger Mitchell's daughter."

Alvarez smiles widely then breaks into a menacing laugh that intensifies when he locks onto the horror-stricken face of his attorney. "Don't worry, Mr. Howard, if we don't get the baby through the CPS adoptive process, and Benton and Celia Brettenvue get the baby through the court system, I will prevail in the end. There are outstanding debts owed me by Señor Brettenvue. I will call them in soon—very soon, but first."

Denver, Colorado

Attorney Stuart Howard shuts his office door and locks it behind him. He drags himself across the room, flops onto his desk chair, and begins shaking. He leans his elbows onto his thighs, drops his head into his hands and rubs them fitfully through his hair. Within minutes his shaking is accompanied by tears and dry heaving. Before leaving the ADX Supermax that morning, Stuart Howard was ordered by his court appointed client to make a phone call. The decision to make the call—or to not make the call—will have deadly consequences. Either way Stuart Howard will be damned for all eternity.

The young attorney never planned on representing the scum of the earth, just the opposite in fact. His legal expertise is international and immigration law and his client base is comprised of hard-working immigrants. Stuart believes in his work and it is a source of great pride for him and his family, or at least it was. When the Federal Government shackled Antonio Alvarez inside the maximum security prison in Florence, they shackled Attorney Stuart Howard to the crime lord. The Law Offices of International Affairs, where the young attorney toils was put on notice—provide legal representation for Antonio Alvarez or close your office doors. By the shit luck of the draw, Stuart's close proximity to the prison and his fluency in Spanish sealed the unholy alliance between the men. He tried to get out of the assignment before it began, and to extricate himself after he met with Alvarez, but the Feds would have none of it. Antonio Alvarez is Stuart Howard's client, and hours ago, that client gave the attorney a directive…

"Call this number. Put a 'don't stop' hit on Gretchen Mitchell."

Alvarez smiled at the defiant look on the young attorney's face, "Mr. Howard, if you do not make the call by the end of business today you will find your wife and two young children dead when you return home. Do you understand?" Stuart heaves over a wastebasket as the Devil's words loop through his head. "Do you understand your choice, Attorney Howard? Gretchen Mitchell dies or your family dies. Do you understand your choice, Attorney Howard? Gretchen Mitchell dies or your family dies. Do you understand your choice, Attorney Howard? **Gretchen Mitchell dies or your family dies.**"

The attorney gathers his thoughts and readies himself for the damnable act he is about to commit. He places pen to paper and writes an account of what happened at the ADX Supermax Penitentiary that morning. He details the demand made by Alvarez that a hit be put on Gretchen Mitchell, the phone number of the contract killer, the threat made against Stuart's wife and children if he refused Alvarez's order, the plan Alvarez has to get Dominique's baby from Child Protective Services in Pennsylvania, and the admission by Alvarez that he has leverage over Benton Brettenvue that will ensure the Peruvian crime lord gets custody of the baby. The written account ends with the damnation of Stuart Howard's soul for putting a "don't stop" assassination order on Gretchen Mitchell.

Stuart Howard keystrokes his computer for the address of Mitchell and Morgan, Attorneys at Law in Philadelphia, Pennsylvania. He folds the paper, places it into an addressed and stamped envelope, and asks his paralegal to join him in his office. "Miss Danvers, go put this in the mailbox in front of the office building. Let me know when you have completed that task." He returns to his desk and waits; it is a short wait.

"Mr. Howard, the envelope is in the mailbox as you requested."

"Thank you, Miss Danvers. That is all for today."

After disconnecting from the paralegal Stuart calls the contract killer, "I have a message, a request from Mr. Alvarez."

"Who is this?"

"Stuart Howard."

"What's the message?"

"Don't stop until you get Gretchen Mitchell. She's a lawyer at Mitchell and Morgan in Philadelphia, Pennsylvania."

One hour later, with his belly full of booze and a bottle of newly prescribed anxiety meds, Attorney Stuart Howard, age thirty-seven, a graduate of Yale Law, husband of Cynthia Warren, father of 2-year-old Hillary and 3-month-old Henry, puts a gun into his mouth and pulls the trigger.

He's the bomb!

Gretchen Mitchell places a call to the firm's research department and asks that the hipster kid be sent to her office. She knows Researcher Randy will come bounding in within minutes and will do anything she asks him to do.

"Yo, I heard you want to see me, Miss Mitchell?"

"Yes, have a seat, Randy." Gretchen gets up from her chair and walks around her desk. She leans her hip onto its corner. "I need some research done on personnel at LewPen. I know this doesn't fall within the normal purview of assignments you get from the firm, and I am aware that it crosses an ethical line or two, but I also know you are the one who can complete the task, without any kerfuffle, so to speak."

The hipster nods, and smiles, really big. "Pish, you can't even begin to fathom what I can do without kerfuffleling, Miss Mitchell."

Gretchen laughs. "Probably best we keep it that way."

"Damn straight, Miss Mitchell."

"This is the situation. One of our clients is experiencing some difficulties with respect to her incarceration. There is an employee at LewPen who needs to be researched and cleared before I am at liberty to request his assistance. Anything you find on him should remain between the two of us."

He nods.

Gretchen goes around her desk, gets a slip of paper and hands it to the young researcher. The paper contains her sex play prison guard's name, Malcolm Price, and the specifics for the research – date of birth, address, marital status, and financials.

Researcher Randy reads the name on the paper, and then, there is silence. An unusual occurrence, for sure.

"Is something wrong, Randy?"

He shakes his head, gets up without further comment, and sprints out of her office calling over his shoulder, "Gotta bounce, get it?"

"What? Get what?"

LewPen

Dominique is pacing her tiny concrete home. She knows it is a prison cell—she hasn't yet turned the corner toward insanity—but for the sake of her unborn baby she pretends her 8x8 is a lovely room at a seaside villa in the South of France. In the few months since her incarceration Dominique has learned little tricks to help pass the time. She sings her baby lullabies in French and English, and she takes her baby girl for daily walks around the cell, telling her about the things they would see if they were in the great outdoors. "Today, mon cheri, we'll visit a magnificent palace in Fontainebleau, stroll through beautiful gardens, and lunch together by a lovely lake. Oh, sweet baby, such beauty awaits us."

Dominique plays a little game for herself, too. It's a sort of a — would you rather this or would you rather that — game of choice. She's played many, many rounds, asking herself…

"Would you rather have ice cream or cake? … Ice Cream … Would you rather have a garden wedding or one in a cathedral? …Neither … Would you rather go for a swim or a hike? … A swim. In the waters of the Belize Barrier Reef." The lonely prisoner gives each question considerable thought before giving an answer. On occasion, a question and an answer surprises her. "Would you choose Alvarez or Fiancetti as the baby's father? … Manuel." On occasion, an answer eludes her. "Would you rather have a fluff down pillow or a fluff down comforter?" No matter the number of times she's posed this question, she hasn't given an answer. Simply stated, she just cannot choose between the two. Of all the niceties of life that are no more, the things BOP-PA-555925 misses most are a soft pillow to rest her head upon, and a warm blanket to cuddle beneath. Neither of those niceties came with her concrete slab.

When sleep fails to claim Dominique, like it did the previous night, she lies awake thinking of what she will name her baby girl. She knows whoever adopts the baby will choose a name for her, but she figures she can name her baby, too. During her sleepless nights she tosses out three names, and when morning comes, she chooses one and uses it throughout that entire day. She begins the process anew when it's lights out and sleep denies. This morning her baby's name is Charlotte. "I think I'll call you Charly for fun."

The prisoner scoffs at that notion, "There was no shortened version of my name, no pet name, no nickname used in the Brettenvue household." Somehow, a sweet memory of playing Hide 'n Seek with her father tries to break through—she pushes it back to the recesses of her mind and focuses on what became of the Brettenvues. "I was barely out of single digits when things became strained between them, and barely out of my teens when *friends* from foreign lands came to visit and..." The young woman breaks out into a cold sweat and receives a swift kick from her baby. She places her hand upon her belly and swirls reassuring circles as she speaks softly, "You mustn't fear. There will be no visits with Celia or Benton, or from any of their *friends*. They **will never** get anywhere near you. Mommy promises, my sweet little one."

Mitchell and Morgan

For the fifth time, Gretchen Mitchell reads the report Researcher Randy forwarded her.

> **Malcolm Price**. <u>Date of birth</u>: September 5, 1982, age 37; <u>Address</u>: 275 Market Street, Lewisburg, Pennsylvania; <u>Marital status</u>: single, never been married; <u>Net Worth</u>: $480 Million.

> **The** Malcolm Price, retired from the NBA in 2013, after suffering a career-ending knee injury. He played ten years for the San Antonio Spurs, bringing his team to two NBA championships in 2005 and 2007. He graduated valedictorian from Bucknell University in 2003, with an undergraduate degree in history and political science, played basketball in the NCAA Division 1 tournament games for four years before beginning his pro-ball career. And he is the bomb!

Gretchen laughs. "Seems Researcher Randy is a fan of Mr. Malcolm Price." The very intrigued lawyer swivels her chair and keystrokes her computer — gasps at the number of articles on the man. "Who the hell are you? Better question, why have I never heard of you?" She does a bit of math, "He's 37. I'm 32. He started his professional career right out of college, so … he was twenty-one … I was sixteen. I certainly wouldn't have heard of him back then, but … I must have heard his name in 2005 or 2007 … I was … eighteen and twenty … and an ungraduated at UPenn … and running track … and living abroad during the summers

… and clearly oblivious." She reads a *Liberty Rings* newspaper article about the 2003 draft pick from The Burg, then gets back to Researcher Randy's report.

> Price lives on the top floor of a converted factory building across from Hufnagle Park, purchase price, $3 Million. Other real estate: Wyldwood Ranch in Wyldwood, Texas, estimated value: $9 Million. Owns: a Magnetite Black Mercedes AMG GT R roadster and a black Land Rover. Recent graduate of UPenn, Master's in Government and Public Policy.

"Nice taste in rides, nice taste schools," she laughs. Then smiles wide at the final bit of information.

> He donates time and money to inner city youth educational and sports programs.

Gretchen leans back in her chair. She isn't normally surprised by the people she meets, but she is very surprised by Malcolm Price, and very curious. "Why on earth is a former professional athlete, a multi-millionaire to boot, working as a correctional officer at a woman's penitentiary?"

What were you expecting?

Malcolm Price races from the penitentiary to his Land Rover after changing into sweats and a long-sleeved T-shirt. He finds there's no need for his jacket as the spring air is unusually warm and balmy. He weaves through the parking lot, tosses himself and his jacket inside his ride and hurries away from LewPen. A lovely lady is expecting his arrival and he has no intention of keeping her waiting. Within minutes Malcolm pulls the Land Rover to a stop in front of his childhood home located in the roughest section of The Burg. He hops from his vehicle and takes the four front steps all at once. "Mama Girl, you ready to go?" he hollers.

"Keep your pants on Malcolm," his Mama Girl hollers back.

Bertha King Price is Malcolm's mother. She is the only family Malcolm has and the only family he has ever needed. She was born and raised in Savannah, Georgia, a descendant of a man sold off a slave ship in Wright Square. Bertha is a proud woman who takes her stock from working hard, earning a fair wage, and banking whatever coins aren't needed, "For a roof over, and food on," as she used to say. When Bertha Price found herself pregnant at seventeen by a man outside her race and standing, she packed her few belongings in a brown paper bag and bought a bus ticket to Pennsylvania.

"Mama Girl, tell me again why we live in Lewisburg and not Philadelphia," a young Malcolm asked more times than need be.
"Because I forgot where the Bell is located, son. Now bother me some of another topic."

Malcolm never believed the story about the Liberty Bell. He's always known his Mama Girl to be a keen learner of history, and figured she'd tell him one day the real reason why she came to Lewisburg. Whatever her reason, Bertha King Price built a nice life for herself and her son, eventually buying the row house that she refuses to leave – even now, when her health is in decline. Today, like three times each week, Malcolm goes back to the hood, gets his Mama Girl and takes her to dialysis treatments. He sits with her through the four-hour ordeal regaling her with stories from the penitentiary. So far, CO Price hasn't shared stories about his steamy sex play with the gorgeous counselor.
After his mother's treatments, Malcolm takes her wherever she wants to go. Most often, she wants to go to the park across the street from his apartment building. Bertha likes looking at the brick and mortar symbol of her son's

success. While she sits a bit with her boy, she spends time telling tales about the people from the neighborhood, and when the gossip flows to a trickle, Bertha retells the story about former Police Chief Gordon Hufnagle, the man for whom the park they enjoy is named. Today, is no different.

"In 1972," Bertha begins as she always does, "Hurricane Agnes unleashed her unholy hell from the Yucatan Peninsula to Iceland, wreaking havoc and destroying anything and anyone in her path. In Lewisburg, Hurricane Agnes is referred to as Agnes Flood because of the intense flooding the hurricane caused of the Susquehanna and Lackawanna Rivers. Chief Hufnagle, a right fine man, died saving lives during the Agnes Flood, and this open-space park is named in his honor. A right thing this borough did for that man"

When his mother finishes her story, Malcolm teases, "Mama Girl, you tell the story like you lived it. You didn't step foot in Lewisburg near a decade after Agnes Flood."

To which his Mama Girl replies, "I didn't land on the moon, neither, but I can tell you the story about Neil Armstrong. Now be quiet boy."

Malcolm is smiling big at today's back and forth with his mother when he sees a Diamond White Mercedes drive past his apartment building. He knows the car is hers before he sees the swing of her platinum hair. Malcolm takes hold of his mother's arm, "Mama Girl, do you mind if we cut this visit short? I just remembered there's someone I need to take care of."

The sun is setting when Malcolm rolls his Land Rover into the parking garage beneath the eight-story brick building at 275 Market Street. Gretchen watches from a side street near the back end of Hufnagle as lights fill the top floor of the former factory. She waits a few minutes before pulling her Mercedes to the curb across the street from the building. "He lives in a penthouse overlooking Hufnagle Park. It stands to reason he'll look out his windows at some point," the lawyer presents her logic.

Malcolm peers down at her car, makes eye contact with the unexpected, yet very welcome visitor, and motions toward the ground. Gretchen follows his gesture and watches as the underground garage door opens. She bangs a U-turn and drives in then sits in her idling Mercedes waiting for his next signal. It comes in the form of a knock on her window. Gretchen lowers it, her light citrusy smell escaping into the balmy night. Malcolm bends his 6'5" frame and leans his arm on the roof of her car. "Get lost going home the other day, Counselor?" He says through a million-watt smile.

Gretchen matches his million-watt smile with one of her own, "I need a favor."

"I hope that's code for your wanting me to bang your brains out," Malcolm playfully growls.

Gretchen tosses her platinum hair, and with a laugh, "I have every intention of banging your brains out, but I do need a favor."

Malcolm stands tall and points to a space next to his Mercedes. "Park your Diamond White next to my Magnatite Black, but don't get out of your car unless you're sure about us." Malcolm is leaning against his car when She. Steps. Out. He is taken aback by her appearance. Gone is the lawyer's pencil-skirt-blazer-combo to which he's become accustomed. This vixen is wearing a peak-a-boo white gauze peasant shirt, pair of bootcut, hip hugging jeans, and pair of scuffed ankle high, stiletto heel cowboy boots. A smile creases his face. "Well, look at you. Just when I thought I had you all figured out, you go and shake it all up. Damn you're one fine piece of work, Gretchen."

"Gretchen" damn near falls off her stilettos when Malcolm Price says her name. She's heard about the sexual swoon before, but she's **never** felt any such thing—until that very second. The quivering woman decides right then and there she likes the swoon. She steps to Malcolm, places her hand into his outstretched gigantic paw and follows him to his place. The eventual lovers ride a privacy elevator to the top floor. Not a word is spoken, but their entwined hands and surveying looks speak volumes.

Gretchen gasps when the elevator door opens into Malcolm's penthouse apartment. She kicks off her ankle boots. He removes her jacket. She pauses at the doorway for a minute taking in the expanse of the space. Then, she begins gushing. "This is *beautiful*. The open floor plan is magnificent. I love the exposed brick walls and the heavily treaded wide-plank floors, and the floor to ceiling windows are imposing, almost frighteningly so, and the furniture—it's so classic yet comfortable."

"You sound surprised."

"I am," Gretchen admits.

"What were you expecting? Black lacquer, chrome and leather?" Malcolm playfully challenges.

"No. No. But I wasn't expecting to see my furniture in your place, either Mr. Price." Gretchen points at select pieces of furniture. "That rolled arm, high back sofa with button-tufted cushions, I have it in white, and that mid-century sloped armchair, I have it in green apple, and the distressed wood end tables and sideboard I have them in medium oak. Your color choices are different, but the furniture in this room is an exact match to mine."

Gretchen stops assessing furniture and studies the man leaning against a brick wall – his legs are crossed at the ankles, his warm caramel-colored eyes are slightly hooded, and his lips have a devilish grin on them. She moves toward him. "Honestly, if you take me to your bedroom and there's a king-sized platform wingback bed with antique silver nail trim, I'll figure I'm in my own bed enjoying another fantasy about you, Mr. Price," she boldly admits.

"King-sized platform wingback bed with bronze nail trim. And since I'm going to turn your fantasy into a reality, you should call me Malcolm." He pushes off the wall and takes one long-legged step forward. He wraps his arm around Gretchen's back at her waist and pulls her to him. He lifts her against his chest and kisses her long and deep then swings her into his arms and heads to the bed Gretchen described to perfection. The woman laughs when she sees the man's room. Her laugh fades when he places her on the bed, his lust bulging hard. Adrenaline pumps through her and she begins to shake.

He smiles wide, "I figured you were a tease. You don't do this sort of thing much, do you?"

Gretchen shakes her head. "No, but don't go spreading that rumor, I have a reputation to uphold."

"Who are you trying to fool with this supposed reputation, Gretchen?"

"Granger Mitchell, of course. Daddy doesn't think any man is good enough for me, so I let him think I try a few men on for size and toss them into the discard pile. It makes Daddy happy that I agree with him."

Malcolm's smile widens. "I'm sure your daddy is gonna love that you're trying me on for size."

Gretchen laughs. "Yes, well, I've never been with a man like you, Malcolm."

"Black?"

"Bald."

Malcolm laughs big. He steps toward the woman on his bed, and extends his hand. She takes hold of it and leaves his bed.

"Where are we going?" she asks, fearful he's changed his mind.

"Let's take a shower. There's something I want to show you."

If I live through it.

Malcolm's shower is a designated room. It's graphite tiled, has a double-wide shower with etched glass doors, and hand-rubbed bronze fixtures. There are dual shower heads, wall jacuzzi jets, and a built-in tile seat. Malcolm reaches in and turns on the waterworks, then closes the door.

"I can see why you wanted to show me the shower. It's wonderful," Gretchen coos.

"That's not what I wanted to show you, Gretchen." Malcolm runs his fingers down her arms and takes one of her hands in his. He places it on his erection and directs her hand down its length. "I'm big."

Gretchen stammers, "Ya think? What the hell am I supposed to do with **that**?"

Malcolm laughs. "It takes some getting used to, but I'm sure you can handle it. Do you use protection?"

"The pill. Do you use condoms?"

Malcolm points to his erection, "Too big, but I'm clean." He reads her questioning eyes. "Gretchen, there are two things you should know about me. I am a man of my word, and I give you my word that I'm never going to do anything to hurt you." He waits for her nod. "When was the last time you had sex? And by that I mean real sex, Gretchen, not rumor-mill sex," he smiles.

"Two years ago on my thirtieth birthday. To be perfectly honest, I barely remember the event," she says with a shrug.

Malcolm raises his hands and gently brushes Gretchen's hair from her face— captures her attention. "Woman, you're going to remember this event."

"If I live through it," she deadpans.

Malcolm pulls his long-sleeved T-shirt over his head, to an audible gasp from Gretchen. She touches his hairless chest. Her fingers tremble and she pulls a choppy breath. She explores his form with starts and stops. Malcolm hooks his fingers into the waistband of his sweats and briefs and pulls. Gretchen doesn't gasp when she sees the full of him because Gretchen can't breathe. No air is going in, no air is going out. Her tremble turns to a full-on shake.

The MAN closes the space between them. He traces the outer edge of her cheek down to her chin and lifts it. He locks eyes with her. "If you need to stop, you need to tell me. I don't want to hurt you, Gretchen."

She nods.

He lifts her peasant top up and over her head. A guttural moan escapes at the sight of Gretchen's breasts more than filling a lacy pink number. He traces the swell of them – his touch eliciting a budding response. Gretchen unhooks the demi-bra unleashing her girls. He gently sweeps the straps from her shoulders, lets the silk fall away as he runs his fingers down her sides to the band of her jeans. He unbuttons them and slides them over her hips. She wiggles them down her long, long legs. He groans at the sight of her pink lace thong before sliding it off.

Malcolm lifts Gretchen onto his waist, wrapping her long legs around him. He walks them into the shower. As they are wetted, Gretchen unwraps her legs and slides herself down until her feet find floor. He steps her back against the shower wall, bends to kiss her. She presses her chest to his and leaves feathery soft kisses across his neck and chest before raising her head and surrendering to his waiting lips. The time they share beneath the warm water is one of exploration, of gentle soapy touches and tender kisses. They step from the shower, wrap themselves in thick towels, and walk to the bedroom hand in hand. Gretchen lets her wrap fall away as she crawls onto Malcolm's bed. She turns to face him just as his towel hits the floor. He joins her, takes her hands and twines their fingers together; he lifts her arms above her head and lowers himself on top of her keeping most of his weight from pressing her down. He gently sweeps her wet hair from her face, rolls a few strands between his fingers. "Your hair, it's wavy and your eyes are blue, but not like any blue I've seen before."

Gretchen appreciates his notice of them, "They're cornflower blue."

"They're beautiful." Malcolm bends and kisses every inch of her, keeping a watchful eye on her cornflowers as they hood and begin to lose focus. Gretchen relaxes into her lover's touch, and when she is ready she welcomes him as he inches in. When he hits a place of resistance he pulls back and waits for Gretchen's desire to welcome him deeper. It is torture waiting to claim her and unwind her, but he gives her the time she needs to adapt to him. When Gretchen opens all of herself and begins begging him with her hips and her orgasmic moans, he presses her deep and empties himself.

Malcolm rolls onto his back and pulls Gretchen on top of him. He tucks her still wet hair behind her ears and stares into her cornflower blues, "Did I hurt you?"

"Hurt me, no. Stretch the hell out of me, yes." Gretchen kisses Malcolm's chin. "Thank you for being so patient in getting me there."

A small groan rumbles from the man. "Woman, you're gonna undo me if I don't watch myself." After a quick catnap, the satiated lovers head to the kitchen for sustenance. Gretchen scrambles eggs with feta cheese and spinach, Malcolm opens a bottle of Señor Sangria Classic

White. They sit across from each other, she dressed in one of his long-sleeved T-shirts that hits her mid-thigh, he in a pair of sweats that hang l.o.w. on his hips.

"Why do you work at the prison?" she asks.

"Penitentiary," he corrects.

"Seriously, Malcolm, I'd like to know why."

"Are you asking me why I work at all or why I work there in particular?"

"There."

"I'm at the women's wing of the penitentiary because there are too many men behind bars who would love to make a name by killing a former NBA star."

Gretchen nods. "Now for the other question, why are you working a nine to five job at all?"

"I have plans for later in life, so while I wait for later, I'm earning an honest day's pay for an honest day's work."

"Do you feel like sharing what your 'later in life' plans are?"

"Politics," is all he says.

"Really?" Gretchen says a bit too quickly and holding the *eeeee* a tad too long.

"You seem surprised, Gretchen."

"Well, yeah, you're way too nice for politics, although you're banging hot, so you'll get the women's vote."

Malcolm smiles. "What makes you think I'm way too nice, Counselor?"

"You loved me gently," Gretchen whispers.

Malcolm gets up from the table and takes Gretchen's hand. "Come on, Woman, I want to gentle you some more."

After an evening of exploration and enthrallment, Malcolm walks Gretchen to her car. It's shortly before 5 AM. He does not want her to leave. She does not want to leave. He squeezes her hand before she slips into Diamond White, "It's a two-and-a-half-hour drive and you've been up most of the night, Ms. Mitchell."

"I believe **you** were the one **up** most of the night, Mr. Price. I was the one pressed tight beneath you, remember?"

"I remember, Woman, and don't change the subject." he growls.

"I have a 10 AM meeting. I can't go looking like this." She pecks his cheek, slides into Diamond White, and eases from the parking space, stopping when he taps her window.

"You never asked me the favor."

"Oh, it's nothing, really." During her post-coital bliss Gretchen decided that she didn't want to sully their night by asking him to do something untoward. "Really, Malcolm forget it."

"Counselor."

She assesses. She realizes this would be a losing battle. She tells him. "I need to get a message to Dominique Brettenvue."

"What's the message?"

"Her parents are petitioning for custody of her baby. If she doesn't express opposition soon, it will be too late."

"Isn't your father's firm representing Celia and Benton Brettenvue?" Malcolm asks notably confused.

"Yes."

"And by helping Dominique you're going against your father?" Malcolm asks, notably concerned.

"Yes."

Malcolm shakes his head. "Like I said last night—just when I thought I had you all figured out, you go and shake it all up. Damn you're one fine piece of work, Gretchen."

The swooning Gretchen winks, smiles, and tosses her platinum hair before letting Diamond White roar out of the parking garage.

There is no defense.

Granger Mitchell has been standing at his front window since 5:30 AM hoping to see Gretchen's Mercedes roar down Old Estate Road. He noticed it was missing from the side drive of her Carriage House when he plugged in his coffee percolator at 5:15. Worry is taking root as his words from the day before bang inside his head…

"You want me to try to get a message to Dominique at the Federal penitentiary?"

"Yes. I hear that you have certain wiles with men that you may be willing to use."

"Yes, well, outside a Federal penitentiary perhaps, but isn't this sort of thing frowned upon?"

"Yes, so don't screw it up."

The father offers a warranted rebuke. "You should not have asked Gretchen to compromise herself in this way—or in any way." The lawyer offers a rational defense; "Gretchen has been going to the penitentiary for weeks, people there know who she is, and with whom she is trying to meet. Asking her to get a message to Dominique Brettenvue would be frowned upon, but it is far from illegal."

The father stops the lawyer. **"There is no defense."** He stops at the windows. They hold no sign of his daughter. "Gretchen, where are you? Did you meet someone of interest or are you doing my dirty work?" The head of the law firm expected his employee to get a message to Dominique during her next Wednesday visit. The father of a dutiful daughter should have known better. "Of course she was going to handle this right away. Gretchen bends to your will—she needs to please."

In the beat of a heart, Dominique Brettenvue, pushes into his headspace. "Another daughter who bent to her father's will— look where that got her." The similarities between the girls smack him hard—both were raised in privilege by very power men—very influential fathers who had expectations for their children. "But we're different," he placates himself with a memory…

"Your birthday is fast approaching. Is there something special you would like, Gretchen?"

"A mother. My mother."

His 8-year old's words landed heavy in his heart. "Yes. Well. If I could manage that for you I most assuredly would."

"You can do anything, Daddy, and if you would do this I will have a mother who can take me to the Mother-Daughter Tea at school. I **have** to attend, but without a mother I will have to attend alone," she teared up at the words and carried them with her as she crawled into bed.

The heavyhearted father tucked his daughter in with a kiss to her cheek and a whispered, "I'm sorry."

On the morning of the Tea, the towering man walked into Wheaton Academy not sure how his daughter would react. Her crestfallen face brightened like the morning sky when she saw him arrive at the gymnasium-turned-Russian Tea Room for a spot of tea with his young daughter.

She smiled and chose Chamomile for them both.

She loved it.

~

"Gretchen, choose a charity for your summer service project."

"For the whole summer?" she eked.

"Yes. You're 16-years old now. People your age work during the summer."

"For money," she pushed.

"You are not in need of money. You are in need of reaping the rewards of helping others. This isn't optional, Gretchen, I expect you to do this, moreover, it's part of your high school curriculum."

She sulked. She chose Habitat for Humanity.

She loved it.

~

"Gretchen, it isn't wise to let your heart lead you anywhere. Use logic and reason as your guideposts ...

as far as I am concerned, Gretchen Rae Mitchell, no man will ever be good enough for you."

The well-intending, completely over-reaching father took the age-old adage that all fathers believe about their daughters, and turned it into a weaponized prophecy. "Gretchen doesn't even try to have a meaningful relationship because she knows I will never approve of anyone." With each and every step he takes, it is accompanied by deeper reflection and harsher self-admonishment. "Gretchen is 32-years old and has never had a romantic relationship. She works sixty hours a week, has few friends, and no time to spend with any of them. Gretchen's life consists of three places, the Cottage on Old Estate Road, the Carriage House on Old Estate Road, and the Law Offices of Mitchell and Morgan." He gathers his thoughts and makes a vow, "This ends today!"

The worrying father steps back to the window and stays there until he sees Gretchen's Mercedes creep toward the Carriage House just before 9 AM. He uses the cell phone he's been carrying since early that morning to call his assistant. "Faye, she's home. Please push my morning meetings to the afternoon. I'll be in soon." He goes to the kitchen, grabs a cup of coffee, and heads upstairs to prepare for a long-overdue conversation with his daughter.

Gretchen feels a pang when she sees her father standing at the window. His solitary image hits her with feelings she'd had only once before…

Gretchen walked into her father's open arms, "Thank you for helping me move, Daddy."

"Walking your things across the back yard barely counts as helping you move, and hardly warrants a thank you."

She smiled through tears, "Then thank you for the Carriage House. I must say, the 2-bedroom place is a bit cramped when compared to your sprawling 6-bedroom, 5-bath estate., but the gesture is just lovely."

"Happy thirtieth birthday, Gretchen."

"Thank you, Daddy. Now, is there any chance you'd consider a swap? This lovely Carriage House for the Cottage?"

He kissed her forehead, "Good night, Gretchen."

"Good night, Daddy."

Hurts so good.

BOP-PA-555925 thinks the Correctional Officer is in her cell to conduct a prevention search. He's not. CO Price points to a far wall. "Go stand there, please."

She does as she is told.

As he moves about the room, he steps onto the stack of yellow envelopes on the floor by her slab, "accidentally" scattering them across the floor. He points, "Your correspondence is unopened."

Dominique nods.

"They should be opened, they are important."

"How do you know they are important?" Dominique snaps.

"We scan prisoner's mail before delivery. You know the protocol."

Dominique nods. "What's in the envelopes?" she asks, her curiosity piqued.

"Your parents want your baby."

Dominique blanches and sways.

The CO goes to her immediate aid. He leads her to her slab, seats her gently, puts his hand to the back of her head and guides it toward her knees. "Stay put." He heads to the toilet/sink/bubbler unit, wets a wad of toilet tissue and places the cold, disintegrating mess onto the back of the prisoner's neck. "Do you need to go to the infirmary?" he asks kindly as he takes her pulse.

Dominique shakes her head. "No, I need to keep my baby away from my parents, from Mr. and Mrs. Brettenvue, she corrects." Dominique raises her head to reveal eyes that are filled with fear.

Malcolm nods. "You need to meet with Gretchen Mitchell, the visiting attorney."

She shakes her head rapidly. "She works for Mitchell and Morgan, so she works for my parents."

"You **need** to meet with Gretchen Mitchell, the visiting attorney—on Wednesday." He bends and gathers the yellow envelopes and places them onto the slab next to BOP-PA-555925. "You **need** to read these, all of them," he says before leaving mother and unborn child alone in their cell.

Mitchell and Morgan
Gretchen's paralegal, Brett Fitzgibbons, is waiting for her outside Conference Room 2B. He is wearing an anxious expression on his face and a hole through the carpet.

"Brett, is there a problem?"

The young man hands Gretchen a piece of navy monogrammed stationery. "He's waiting in his office for you. He came in late and pushed back three meetings."

Gretchen shoves her case files at Brett and high tails it to the eighth floor. She pulls herself to a stop inches from her father's assistant, Faye Smith, a perfectly coiffed, exquisitely dressed, supremely professional guard dog.

"My father is expecting me, Mrs. Smith."

"Yes, Miss Mitchell." Mrs. Smith stands from her seat and walks seven feet to Granger Mitchell's door. She knocks three times and waits.

"Send her in," booms the voice from within the inner sanctum.

Mrs. Smith opens the door for Gretchen then pulls it closed behind her.

"Good morning, Daddy," Gretchen chippers.

"Did you take care of the matter we discussed, yesterday?"

"I believe so."

"Ambiguity does not suit you, Gretchen. You either did or you did not take care of the matter." Granger rises from his chair and imposes his stature and authority simply by standing near her. Sort of.

"Huh."

"Huh, what?" her father asks.

Gretchen thinks it's best not to tell her father he's less imposing now that she's spent the night with the MAN, so she offers a response to his original line of inquiry. "I presented my request for a favor. It is up to the person to decide if he is capable of granting it."

Granger points to a chair. "Sit, will you?"

She is very surprised her father phrased his directive as a question. Gretchen crosses her ankles, folds her hands, and places them in her lap.

"You were out all night. Did that circumstance have anything to do with the favor?" Granger watches his daughter's face.

"Partly," she offers.

"Ambiguity does not suit you Gretchen," Granger repeats.

"Yes, I believe you said that. The thing is, Daddy, I have met someone with whom I enjoy spending time. I know how you feel about this subject, so I think ambiguity is my best option."

Granger nods, then smiles. "Yes, about that. This morning I was thinking perhaps the next time you embark on a relationship I should meet the young man."

Gretchen blanches, breaks into a sweat, and produces enough adrenaline to render her a shaking mess. "You...You want...You want to meet my gentleman friend?" She croaks. "*This*, gentleman friend?" She croaks for a second time.

"That is my intent, but apparently there's a reason you object to that suggestion," Granger stares at his daughter.

The daughter begins shaking her head. "No. No. There's no reason why you shouldn't meet him. I mean, that is what fathers do, right? They meet their daughter's suitor, to make sure they are suitable, right?"

"I see I have failed you, Gretchen. We should have done this ages ago, perhaps then you wouldn't be in such a kerfuffle. I think we should continue this discussion another time. You have work to do," he says dismissively.

Gretchen gets up and remains standing near his desk.

Granger looks at her blankly. "Why are you standing there?"

"I'm waiting for my list, you know of the things you want me to do."

"There is no list. I summoned you so we could talk, which we did; you may go."

Gretchen leaves her father's office in a haze. She thinks she may have curtsied before exiting and thinks she may have heard the echo of Mrs. Smith's laugh as she stumbled down the halls of the executive suite.

Brett Fitzgibbons pops from his seat like a Jack-in-the-box, and waves his hand in his boss' direction. Her spell broken, she looks with wondering eyes. He continues his pantomime, waving a telephone receiver, and motioning his boss toward her office. He sends a call to her line.

"Gretchen Mitchell," she announces to the caller.

"Woman, how are you this morning?"

Gretchen's breath hitches and *something* becomes very tingly at the sound of his voice. "I believe John Mellencamp, or John Cougar Mellencamp, or John Cougar, or whomever he may be, wrote a song about my current condition."

Malcom enjoys this woman, "Counselor, I believe you are referencing a #1 hit by Mr. John Mellencamp *Hurts So Good.*"

Gretchen giggles, "I believe you are correct, Mr. Price."

"I want you," Malcolm groans.

"I'm not sure I'm capable of meeting any needs other than talking, Malcolm."

"Then, we talk. Let's do this. All of this, Gretchen. Let's get to know each other, really know each other, while we enjoy each other. It will have to be at my place unless you're ready to introduce me to your daddy." He laughs.

"Actually, he and I just had an interesting conversation about my love life, such as it is."

"Seems we have our first topic of conversation for this evening. What time can you be at my place?"

"Name a time," Gretchen says surprising the hell out of herself.

"Seven."

"Seven." Gretchen disconnects and immediately replays the conversation in her head. She blanches, breaks into a sweat, and produces enough adrenaline to render her a shaking mess for the second time that day. It isn't even noon.

LewPen

Dominique sits crossed-legged on her slab with seven envelopes and seven legal documents spread around her. The first time she saw the words, "Petition for Custody of the Unborn Child of Dominique Brettenvue," she blanched, broke into a sweat, and produced enough adrenaline to render her a shaking mess. She's settled herself some after reading each page of each document, but she isn't feeling quite right. She puts the papers back into the envelopes and stretches out on her back. Normally, she lays upon one side or the other, but this time, she stretches out on her back. She raises one of her arms and places it across her face to block the light that's searing straight to her brain. She gently rubs her belly until her breathing returns to normal and her baby stops cartwheeling inside her. She takes a few quiet minutes, then falls asleep.

Dinnertime coincides with the end of her nap. She is starved *and* she is nauseated. The prisoner retrieves her tray through a slot-opening in the locked door, and takes it to her concrete desk. Still feeling green, she moves the crap-food from one side of the tray to the other. She doesn't want a morsel, but she sits on her concrete stool and begins feeding her baby.

Mews to moans.

Malcolm has been waiting outside for Gretchen for nearly an hour. He is leaning back against the brick frontage of 275 Market Street – blending into the night around him. He is dressed from head to toe in black—his wool cap, his Armani jacket, his jeans, his signature kicks—all black. A stark contrast to the all-white woman he's expecting. He pushes off the brick front, and key fobs the garage when he sees Diamond White roar toward him. He motions for her to drive in, then follows her car into the dark space, pausing when something catches his eye. He turns back toward Market Street in time to see a black Escalade inch its way past his building just before the garage door closes shut.

"What are you looking at, Malcolm?" Gretchen asks.

He turns toward his woman's voice. She is standing at her car backlit by sparse lighting. Her bright white platinum hair breaks the darkness around her. As she moves toward him he can see she's wearing a black ribbed turtleneck that barely meets the top of black skinny jeans that barely meet the top of black four-inch stiletto ankle boots.

Gretchen steps slowly toward the man, her movements are halting, hinting that she's unsure he will be there when she gets to him. Her cornflower blues begin to sparkle with desire as she moves through fractured light, her lips spread into a warm smile. The closer she gets to her man the surer she becomes. She takes the final few steps quickly and throws herself into his arms.

Malcolm pulls her tight against him. "You came," he whispers against her cheek.

She pulls her head back and looks up into his eyes. "Yes, three times if memory serves me well."

Malcolm laughs big.

They ride the elevator in silence, their hands tightly entwined, their eyes locked onto one another's. She heads directly to the kitchen when they get inside. He takes their coats and hangs them in a walk-in closet and grabs a Spurs sweatshirt from inside. He hands it to Gretchen. "There's a chill in here."

Gretchen waves her cell in Malcolm's direction. "Do you mind if I make a quick call?"

He shakes his head, "Do you need privacy?"

"No, thanks." Gretchen calls the Granger Mitchell Cottage; it goes directly to voicemail. "Hi, Daddy, I wanted to let you know I won't be returning to the Carriage House tonight, I didn't want you to worry. Have a good evening; I love you, Daddy." When she turns back toward Malcolm, she finds a smile cutting wide across his face, his dimples running deep and long down his neatly trimmed stubbled cheeks.

Gretchen sits at the table and watches the man move through the bronze-and-stainless steel-applianced room. He takes a couple of marinating steaks from the refrigerator to let them get to room temperature and fires up the 2-zone grill on his range. He joins Gretchen at the table taking one of her hands in his. He twines their fingers together.

Gretchen marvels at the size of Malcolm's hand in comparison to hers. "Your fingers are so long."

"You know what they say about men with long fingers." Malcolm smiles wide.

"If they say the length of a man's finger has some correlation with the length of his penis, I can attest truth to that," Gretchen smiles wide.

"Get your head out of the gutter, Woman. They say a man with long fingers is born to play basketball."

"You played basketball?"

Malcolm shakes his head. "You didn't know who I was when you started your sex play at the penitentiary?"

"How would I know such a thing?"

"I don't know, Woman, maybe you have a television or you read a newspaper or a magazine from time to time. I was pro for ten years."

"Yeah, Researcher Randy told me," Gretchen smiles.

"Who is Researcher Randy?"

"He's a hipster kid who works for the firm. He did the research on you. He is **very** impressed by your career. I think he might be one of those crazy fans you ball bouncers get. Until I read his research, I thought you were a prison guard. A rather hot prison guard. By the way, I wasn't kidding when I said you were my co-star in more than a few sexual fantasies. I should thank you for your ..... thoroughness." She smiles and moves from the table and onto his lap.

His response is immediate. "Woman, you need to go sit over there."

Gretchen nuzzles his neck and runs her hand down his chest as she rubs back and forth on his excitement.

"Seriously, Gretchen, I can barely be in the same room with you, let alone have you mounted on me."

The aroused woman wiggles against him, "I think I need you."

He groans. "I know I need you, but I want to get to know you. Let's eat and then sit a while and talk." Malcolm looks deeply into Gretchen's eyes. "Then, I'll gentle you some."

Gretchen smiles wide. "You're going to *gentle* me. Is that our thing, now, because if it is, I love it." She nuzzles into Malcolm's neck again.

After some dinner and easy chit-chat Malcolm leads Gretchen to a space behind his bedroom. The area is expansive and consists of several rooms: a game room, a small theater, a home office, a magnificent guest bedroom suite, and tons of unused space in back.

Gretchen inspects and assesses the areas as she moves through, turning several times while walking each of the rooms, "You own the whole top floor of this building?"

"I own the building."

Gretchen guffaws. "I thought you overpaid for your apartment at $3 Million, you actually made a killing on this building at that price."

"I did," Malcolm nods.

Gretchen hip-chucks him. "Well done, Mr. Price."

"Thank you, Ms. Mitchell." Malcolm takes Gretchen's hand and leads her back to the game room. They sit on a deep leather couch the color of Malcolm's skin. Gretchen finds it as smooth and comfortable as its owner.

"I want to know you, Gretchen." He twines his fingers through hers. "Tell me about your family."

The woman who is perfectly comfortable presenting a case, repositions herself so she's facing him, her long legs crossed in front of her. "My father is my family, but let me start by telling you about my mother." She pulls a long breath, shimmies her shoulders, and begins, "Delaney Rae Hamilton, of Sweetwater, Georgia, met my father at an alumni event at the University of Pennsylvania the year she graduated, and he was seven years out. They married in 1986, and had me in 1987. A year later, my mother died in a plane crash." Gretchen breathes deep when Malcolm gently squeezes her fingers. "My mother was very beautiful. She had hair the color of corn silk, cornflower blue eyes, and push-button dimples. She was way shorter than my 5'11" but other than that I resemble her very much. She's the reason why I bleach and straighten my hair, so I'm different, for my father, you see." This time Gretchen smiles at the gentle squeeze of Malcolm's hand, and becomes quite animated for the next part of her storytelling.

"My father always says Miss Delaney Rae was as smart as they came and as outspoken as she chose. He says she put him in his place many times—but I can't imagine anyone putting Granger Mitchell in his place. My father's parents passed before I was born, so I haven't much to say on that topic. The Hamilton's of Sweetwater never had much to do with my father or me after my mother's death. They blamed Granger Mitchell for not insisting my mother extend her visit back home instead of trying to beat a weather front moving into Philadelphia. It wasn't until many years after the plane crash that one of my mother's cousins admitted my father begged my mother to stay put in Sweetwater. In fact, my parents had words about her flying in bad weather, and he tried to cancel the private plane, but it had already taken off. Even after knowing the truth, the Hamilton's never reached out to us." Gretchen shrugs and continues on.

"Now for Granger Mitchell. My father is a larger-than-life man who commands respect, which is fine, because most always he earns it. He holds me close, mostly out of fear of losing me. In fact, I saw him standing at his window this morning when I rolled in. Apparently, my not returning home last night set him to converse with me on an interesting subject. I told you about my faux reputation with men and the roots of its inception — my Daddy thinking that no man is good enough for me, and my showing him I agree by supposedly trying men on for size and discarding them."

Malcolm nods once. "Go on."

"This morning I was summoned to Granger Mitchell's office. He asked if I took care of the Dominique matter. I told him I believed so. Granger replied, 'ambiguity does not suit you, Gretchen' then he asked whether I was out all night because of the Dominique matter. I told him partly. Again, he mentioned ambiguity. That's when I told him I met someone with whom I enjoy spending time, and that since he has particularly strong opinions about me and romantic relationships, I thought ambiguity was my best option. The two of us were setting upon unchartered waters and I had absolutely no idea where the conversation was heading. Daddy surprised the hell out of me when he said, 'Yes, about that. I think the next time you embark on a relationship I should meet the young man'. I'm telling you, Malcolm, you could have knocked me over with one finger—I know that's just a saying, but in your case it's probably true—but I suppose that discussion is for another time. So, anyway, there I was, a 32-year old woman rendered nearly daft, and mostly mute. Daddy took one look at me and said he should have broached this subject years ago and avoided my present state of kerfuffle."

Gretchen eyes the man sitting across from her. She puts a hand to her hip. "Have you something to say on this particular matter, Mr. Price?"

He lets out the laugh he's been holding. "Woman, you tell the best stories. I think I enjoy talking with you as much I enjoy rendering you speechless."

Gretchen shrugs and moves to the far end of the couch. She nestles between his outstretched legs, leans back against him and wraps his arms around, "It's your turn."

"It's just me and my mother, Bertha King Price, of Savannah, Georgia. Our mothers hail from the same state. Different circumstances, though. Mama Girl, I call her that because she is my mama, but she had me when she was still a girl of seventeen."

Gretchen smiles, "Well isn't that just wonderful!"

He smiles and continues, "I don't know who my father is, but I know he is Caucasian, is considerably older than Bertha, and from a 'different station in life' than Mama Girl. She left Georgia without telling her family about me and I'm not sure if she told the man who impregnated her. Whatever her reasoning, Bertha Price put her belongings into a brown paper bag and boarded a bus to the home of the Liberty Bell. Problem was, she couldn't remember where the Bell was located, so she ended up in Lewisburg. I'm sure that part of Mama Girl's story is fiction. My mother is a learner of history, so I suspect there is another reason why she ended up in Lewisburg."

Malcolm's story thus far receives the sweetest smile and a tighter wrap of his arms around Gretchen.

"Mama Girl and I lived for many years in a fifth-floor walk-up in the projects. We had no family to help us out, so Mama Girl created a family for us. Miss Etta Jones, a single mother of three lived across the hall from us. She and Mama Girl traded off on childcare so they could earn a paycheck. Mama Girl watched me and Etta's kids during the day, and then worked as a secretary at the bus company at night while I stayed at Etta's place. A bonus for Mama Girl was that her boss gave her free bus passes she and Etta used to get back and forth to work and she and I would use to get to Sunday morning services.

"By the time I began high school, Mama Girl had enough money to buy a tiny row house. It's in the roughest section of The Burg, but it's her home. I don't like her living there, but as she reminds me, 'it's none of my never mind'. Three times a week I take Mama Girl for dialysis treatments, and spend the four hours' time telling her stories about my work and listening to her stories about the hood. Mostly, I spend the time thanking the good Lord for my Mama Girl."

Gretchen is overcome with feelings of which she is most unaccustomed. She turns in Malcolm's arms and crawls up onto his lap. She takes his face between her hands, and stares deep. "Malcolm Price, you are a good man."

The 'good man' wraps his arms around Gretchen and flips her beneath him. "I'm gonna press you into this couch, Woman, and show you how good I am." He undresses her slowly then touches every inch of her softly. Her mews undo him. When he can't stand it a minute longer, he lifts her into his arms and takes her to his bed. He eases into Gretchen slowly and softly until her mews turn to moans.

Where's Charlotte?

Dominique is practically dead on her feet, so she stays off her feet. Every time she surrendered to sleep's pull it punished her with hideous nightmares, so in the wee hours, she pushed herself into a sitting position, pressed her back against the concrete wall, and denied her subconscious its punitive drag through Hell. She is finding that even awake, the dreadful dreams find her – claim her…

Dominique was startled when Manuel dropped onto the first-class seat next to her ……. Manuel stood, reached into his pocket, and sat back down. Dominique turned and watched his movements—she wished she hadn't when he showed her the pregnancy test he found discarded back at Hamanasi. "I think we have things to discuss, Dominique."

~

"I need to use the bathroom, Manuel."

When she returned, he noticed the swell of her breasts and tiny baby bump. He felt both during their encounter the night before, but seeing the physical proof of life touched something in him. The deep trenches in his cheeks announced his utter joy at becoming a father—there was no such look on Dominique's face, no sparkle in her eyes.

"Manuel ….. Manuel."

"Sorry, did you say something?"

"I asked if we are getting up for the day?"

The expectant father opened his arms to the expectant mother—a playmate he met on vacation—a person who should be nothing more than a great memory of his time in Belize. And yet… Manuel smiled when she moved into this embrace, and settled in for sleep.

~

Joy Fiancetti paused at a workstation, rested her backside against it, and drummed her fingers on the tabletop. "…Dominique, you probably think that we are going to ask you for the names of the other Realm leaders. We aren't going to ask, but you will be telling us in no time at all."

Dominique laughed. She motioned her head at the white erase boards that held Joy's investigative results. "Look at those boards. You have nothing, and I will give you nothing."

Joy sauntered to Dominique and leaned low. "Oh, but you *will* give us what we want. You overplayed your hand in the Safe House." Joy moved away and paused until the prisoner found her with her eyes. "When you raged at Manuel about your baby, you gave away too much." Joy began roaming the Center again.

Dominique began replaying her words in her head.

Joy helped her out. "I believe you said that the baby is not Manuel's. That it is not a Fiancetti and if you had learned that this baby was a Fiancetti, it would not be in your womb." **The trained FICA agent waited until the prisoner began squirming in her seat. Joy tilted her head back and laughed.** "You should squirm, Dominique. You know your baby is not a Fiancetti. That means you had a paternity test, or at the very least it means that you can count the weeks between missed periods, which means you *know* who the father is." **Joy dropped a bomb of suspicion.** "My guess is that the Baby Daddy is Peruvian crime lord, Antonio Alvarez, who not only sits in a leadership position of The Realm, but is also highlighted on our leadership white board over there."

Dominique shifted and sneered. "You know **nothing**."

Joy snickered. "Oh, Dominique, the truth is written all over your face. You are not cut out for the world of deception. You aren't very good at it. Maybe it's the strawberry-blonde ringlets, and freckles. You just look too damned cute to be a mercenary."

"I deceived every one of you," **she hissed.**

Joy laughed BIG. "Yes, for time you did. Tell me, Dominique Brettenvue, how is the world of deception working out for you now?"

~

Outstretched hands, dozens of hands, clawed at her abdomen trying to get her unborn baby. She screamed at the attackers, "No! No! You will never have her!" **A baby's cry broke the**

73

still of the night. "Charlotte? Is that you?" She touched her flat belly, "Charlotte! Where are you!" A laugh assaulted her then words inflicted a mortal wound.

"Where's **Charlotte?**" he called out. "Did anyone see a little girl with strawberry-blonde ringlets and freckles on her nose, that stands about yay high?" he said as he pulled back a curtain here or looked behind a chair, there. "**Charlotte,** you are getting very good at this hiding game," he said as he opened a closet door or peeked behind the cocktail bar. "There you are sweet girl. Come to Grandpapa."

Dominique frozen in place on the concrete slab, the realization that Benton and Celia Brettenvue want custody of her baby sends waves of terror through her, adding to the fear she already carries that Antonio Alvarez will take her baby. "Neither of those things are supposed to happen," she hisses. "I made a deal with the Fiancettis. I turned against Antonio Alvarez and the others—RFI promised my baby would be placed for adoption and protected from the evil ones," she rages, then gasps at the angry kick from inside. "Charlotte, oh, Charlotte."

The mother who loves her baby takes a slow cleansing breath and swirls little circles on her baby bump. "I lived up to my end of the bargain, mon cheri; it's time for RFI to live up to their end."

Did you ever—even once?

Gretchen is sprawled across Malcolm's chest when she wakes Saturday morning. He has one of his arms across her back, the other across her ass. She wiggles up toward his face and kisses him gently.

"Woman, I'm thinking you could cause me some serious trouble. You feel way too good, way too soon."

Gretchen stiffens at his words then pushes off the bed and heads to the bathroom. The concerned man is leaning against the headboard waiting her return. "What's bothering you, Woman?" He pats the bed next to him.

The woman, wearing one of her man's long-sleeved T-shirts and a frown, joins him on the bed. She nestles into his shoulder and welcomes the wrap of his arms. "I guess I'm at the same place as you. I'm feeling things I've never felt before. On the one hand, I think I should pull all the threads that are hanging from this thing and see what unravels. On the other hand, I want to leave the threads alone and let them wrap and twine in their own way. I suspect you have a better point of reference as to how we should be feeling at this point in a relationship, Malcolm, so I think I'd better defer to your assessment that this feels way to good, way too soon."

Malcolm strokes the nestled woman's hair, runs his hand the length of it, letting the blunt cut ends flick through his fingers. A tactile touch memory of another woman's hair tries to push through. He tries to deny it.

He can't.

"There was a girl who I had a thing with early in my career." He pulls a deep breath, lets it out slowly. "But for the ten years I played with the Spurs, I didn't have the time, or desire to bring a woman along for the ride. Life on the road is difficult. For me, the travel and demands of the sport weren't conducive with the state of monogamy or matrimony." He pauses for a kiss to her head then continues. "When I got injured and my basketball career ended, I needed some time to figure out who I am without the game. I made an unholy mess of myself, and in the process, I nearly destroyed the few relationships that I hold sacred. I eventually figured things out, and made a plan. Now, you're here and I'm reevaluating my plan seeing if you'll fit in and wondering if you'll even want to."

Gretchen pulls a long, slow breath of her own, "So, what should we do?"

"Not we, Gretchen, you."

Gretchen pushes from the man's shoulder and sits to face him. "Me? Why am I in this decision-making place all alone?"

Malcolm puts his black hand onto her white leg. "Did you ever—even once—think you'd choose to be with a black man? Did you ever consider the difficulties of being with a black man? Did you ever consider raising bi-racial children? Because if you haven't, you need to do your thinking, now." Malcolm touches the cheek of a deflating Gretchen. He knows his words landed like a sucker punch and knocked a fair amount of wind out of the woman he wants. He kisses her on the top of her head. "I'm gonna shower, then I need to take Mama Girl for a treatment. I'll be gone about five hours; I'd like you to be here when I get back. Gretchen. I hope you will stay."

Gretchen barely nods.

Market Street

Antonio Alvarez's goon watches Malcolm Price pull out of the underground garage at 275. The contracted assassin can't believe his target is the love toy of The Malcolm Price. "Hope I can kill the puta without taking you out, 77. If not, then that's the 'Price' you'll have to pay," the goon laughs. He slows his ride on the early, empty streets of Lewisburg – cautions himself, "Don't get his attention." The hitman follows the player to Cross Street in the blighted section of the borough. He watches as Price parks at the curb in front of 11-B, a tiny row house, and enters without a knock. "Must be where he grew up. You sure have moved up in the world. Good for you." In minutes Malcolm and his Mama Girl are in his Land Rover and on the move. "Let's see where you two are going so early in the morning."

Philly

Faye rolls from Granger's spoon and pushes herself to a sitting position. "Are you feeling any better about the conversation you had with Gretchen?"

"Once I talked it through with you, yes. I'm glad you had the office monitoring camera engaged. I heard you laugh, by the way, when Gretchen was still in earshot." Granger playfully squeezes Faye's knee.

"Did you see her face? Oh, Granger, it was priceless. The poor thing was all in a doo-dah at the prospect of having her new man meet you. I wonder when that will be?"

"When she figures out whether this one is the one, I suspect," he exhales his words.

Granger reaches for Faye, pulls her back into his spoon and whispers, "Happy twenty-fifth anniversary, Faye. I love you more and more each day."

275 Market Street

Gretchen takes the privacy elevator to the garage level an hour before Malcolm is due home from Mama Girl's dialysis appointment. She unlocks Diamond White and pulls a few things from its trunk. She rests her backside against the Mercedes and replays Malcolm's words. Again. For the last several hours they've banged through her head. Over. And. Over. And. Over. With each loop she pulls apart one of the things he asked her to consider. She is ready to present her findings, so she gives her words a run through.

"Did you ever, even once, think you'd choose to be with a black man? — That's an easy question to answer, **no**. In fairness, I've never thought I'd be with *any* man. Now that the choice is upon me, race has no bearing on my affections. I was drawn to Mr. Malcolm Price the second I saw him, and the attraction has grown deeper. I think I might be falling hard for this man."

"Did you ever consider the difficulties of being with a black man? — That's an easy question to answer, **no**. In fairness, I haven't considered the difficulties of anything. To a fault, and on occasion to my detriment, I am a, by-the-seat-of-the-pants kind of girl. I suspect that is a byproduct of being raised by a brilliant lawyer who drilled that there's nothing too difficult to handle."

"Did you ever consider raising bi-racial children? — This question causes me some concern since I've never considered having children of any race. Since Mr. Malcolm Price raised this issue, he must already know that he wants children. Now what?"

Gretchen is pulled from her ruminating by the lifting of the garage door. She exhales when she realizes the car driving in isn't Malcolm's Land Rover. She checks her watch, waits for the car to pass her by, then sprints to the privacy elevator. When she gets to the penthouse, she tosses a small valise onto the couch and goes directly to the kitchen. She quickly rummages through cabinets and the refrigerator for ingredients then gets to work. The impromptu chef starts with a package of sausage links. She removes the casing and slices the links into rounds and browns them. While they are cooking, she chops an onion and a clove of garlic, and when the sausage is done, she removes the slices from the pan and pours a splash of olive oil in and adds the onion and garlic. She sautés them until they are nicely browned then adds a can of crushed tomatoes, returns the browned sausage, sprinkles in a little salt, ground black pepper, dried basil, dried oregano, and a bay leaf. She sets the sauce to simmer for an hour and heads to the shower.

Wonderful smells greet Malcolm before the elevator door opens. He calls out to Gretchen, checks the kitchen to see what awaits him, then goes in search of his woman. His smile widens when he hears the shower running and her singing the feminist tune, *You Don't Own Me.* Malcolm opens the shower door and steps inside. "Woman, if you'll consent, I'd like to own certain parts of you for a few minutes." He presses her against the wall and owns the hell out of her.

At the sound of the smoke-detector, the lovers race to the kitchen. Both are soaking wet and naked as the day they were born. Gretchen stomps her foot at the sight of her cooked down to practically nothing scorched sauce. Malcolm grabs the pan, puts it under running water, and laughs at his stomping woman. "We can order in or we can go somewhere for dinner."

"Let's order in. I brought a little something-something to wear for you, Mr. Price."

Malcolm follows Gretchen's eyes toward the valise set on the couch. "Vixen Woman, I have a feeling I'm never going to want to leave this apartment again."

Gretchen bats her cornflower blues. "Before the fun and games begin, let's get dressed and talk a while, okay?"

They dress in silence which is broken by the sound of Malcolm's cell. He excuses himself to take the call. When he returns, they go to the game room, the place where they had their first conversation.

Gretchen crawls onto Malcolm, spreads her legs across his lap, and takes a deep cleansing breath. She gently traces the lines of his face playing with his scruff. He notices the tremble in her fingers; an uncomfortable roll starts in the pit of his stomach as he waits for her to begin.

"So, I'm good on your first two questions, but I think we need to discuss raising bi-racial children. Since I've never thought about having children, this is most definitely a talking point. So, let's start off with the big question, do you want to have kids?"

"I'd like to have at least one. What about you, Gretchen, I mean now that you've thought a little about the subject? Are there children in your future?"

"Maybe."

"And if they are bi-racial, how will you address that with them?"

Gretchen pauses. "Malcolm, when you look at me is my being white the first thing you see?"

"Yes."

Air pushes from Gretchen as though it's been sucker punched out of her.

Malcolm takes her hand and playfully squeezes it, "Gretchen, you are the most white person I've ever seen."

"Well, yes. I suppose I am of the shiny white variety, but you very well know what I meant."

"I do, and no, your whiteness isn't the first thing I noticed."

"Okay, and your being black isn't the first thing I noticed."

"And..."

"Well, I think if we teach our kids that skin color shouldn't be the first thing you see about a person, they will be all right."

Malcolm pulls Gretchen tight against him. "Did you just say *our* kids?"

"Well, what do you know, I believe I did." Gretchen laughs big.

Malcolm kisses Gretchen in a way he's never kissed her or any woman before. It is a soul changing kiss for him, "You're gonna undo me, Woman, and I'm glad for it."

After many minutes of just holding one another, Malcolm whispers in Gretchen's ear, "I know you have a little surprise for me, but can we move it to tomorrow; I just want to hold you, tonight."

Gretchen smiles knowing their relationship just took one giant step forward.

Vixen Woman

The man is pleased deep that Gretchen agreed to meet his mother so soon in their relationship.

"Does your mother know anything about me?"

"I told her some, yesterday," Malcolm smiles. "Come on," he offers her his hand and leads her to the door. When they are inside, Malcolm calls out, "Mama Girl, there's company, so don't keep her waiting."

"I'm coming, boy, now hold your demands." Bertha King Price enters her living room and pulls up short.

"Mama Girl, this is Gretchen Mitchell."

Gretchen crosses the small room and extends her hand. "It's a pleasure to make your acquaintance, Miss Price."

Bertha King Price takes a step forward and instead of shaking Gretchen's hand she pulls her in for a hug, "Handshakes are for business deals young lady, hugs are for family."

Gretchen accepts Bertha's embrace, then gives the woman one of her own.

"Sit next to Malcolm so I can watch your expressions and see if you two are feeling equally of things," Bertha directs. She addresses her son, "Malcolm, I believe you understated a few things, Miss Mitchell is as pretty as a sunrise and she is most definitely well on her way to loving you."

"Mama Girl, I believe we discussed this, already," Malcolm admonishes.

"Yes, son, but you are wrong about the intensity of your woman's feelings. Isn't that right Miss Mitchell?"

"Please call me Gretchen, and yes, ma'am, I am certainly on my way to loving Malcolm, but we are very new at this, at least I am. I've never been seriously involved with anyone prior to your son."

"Does your daddy know about my son, Gretchen? Because it's been my experience that some people harbor deep feelings about such things as race in relationships."

"My father knows there is someone in my life. He has expressed a desire to meet my suitor and since Malcolm is apparently ready for family introductions, I think the meeting between the men is imminent."

"And after the meeting, will there be discourse between the men? I ask because I think my son deserves fair warning," Bertha King Price says straight.

Gretchen takes hold of Malcolm's hand. "Someone recently asked me if I had ever considered dating a black man before I began dating a black man. I had not. It never occurred to me to consider race when it comes to matters of the heart. I believe that sentiment is ingrained in me by my father."

Bertha nods. "Malcolm, it pleases me that you have chosen this woman to love. You do right by her, son."

Malcolm crosses the room and pulls his Mama Girl to him.

When they leave two hours later, having been fed and pampered by Mama Girl, she calls out, "Malcolm, if you get that girl pregnant, you better be marrying her."

Malcolm smiles wide at his Mama Girl, "Yes, ma'am, I surely will."

The Penthouse

Gretchen prepares a salad for dinner. She adds some pulled chicken to the top and drizzles it with Ranch dressing – the only one available in Malcolm's kitchen. The man of 275 Market Street has been in his home office since they returned home, and the woman has been camped out in the living room catching up on some very ignored case files. They break for dinner shortly before 8 PM and spend some very quiet moments cleaning the dishes. Malcolm takes hold of Gretchen's wrist when she passes by. "Are we good, Woman?"

"Better than," she smiles.

"Doesn't feel like we're good, Gretchen. Talk to me."

"I think I'm going through pre-withdrawals. I haven't even left and I'm already missing you," she says a noticeable bewilderment attached to her words.

"Can you stay Wednesday night? Maybe work from here after your visit to the penitentiary?"

Gretchen beams. "That's perfect."

Malcolm pats her on the ass. "Now that that's settled; I do believe there is a fashion show in my future."

Gretchen scurries to the bedroom, grabs her valise from the closet, and squeals all the way to the shower.

Malcolm leaves Gretchen to herself and grabs a shower in the guest suite off the game room. He is pressed against the headboard of his king-sized bed when Gretchen struts into the room. The man who had yet to gasp—gasps—then he moans—then he groans.

Vixen Woman stands in the doorway leading to his bedroom wearing a pale blue, push-up-bra-camisole-thong-thing, and nothing else. Her hair is wild and crinkly, her eyes are shadowed darkly, her lips are painted sinfully. She eyes her man seductively. "Tonight, I'm in charge."

Malcolm groans. "Woman what are you…"

"I'm in charge, Malcolm. Do you agree?"

Malcolm smiles w.i.d.e. "Agreed."

"Good, because it's my turn to do a little loving, although I can't promise it will be of the gentle variety." Gretchen channels Vixen Woman as she s.t.r.u.t.s. to the end of the bed and crawls the length of it. She spreads Malcolm's legs as she moves forward. He is clearly ready for whatever she has in mind. "I see you are eager for the fun and games to begin. Skootch down, come on, flat on your back."

Malcolm laughs. "I see Miss Sassy has arrived."

"Further down, Malcolm. Give me your hands." Gretchen puts their hands palm to palm and locks their fingers together. She raises his arms over his head. "Leave them there. You don't touch unless I ask you to." Gretchen straddles Malcolm to a rolling set of moans. She kisses his brows, his cheeks, his lips, she runs feather-soft fingers across his face and shoulders. She lays flat on his chest then rises above him like a mermaid emerging from the sea. She straddles his length, gives it a wiggle, then a press.

Each time she notices movement above his head, she stops until she regains obedience. When she's tortured her man (and herself) sufficiently, she turns around. "Unsnap the thong and follow my lead." Her lead involves kissing, and touching, and mouthing of all kinds. Gretchen doesn't try to take all of her man, but the part she takes gets him ready. She knows he is close when she cups his balls. With an urgent moan, Malcolm flips Gretchen onto her back and pushes in. She cries out and bucks in pain.

The man in the throes presses her to the mattress, her painful cry finally registering with him as he comes down, "Fuck! I hurt you," Malcolm rolls off her. "Come here, Gretchen." She is shaking and trying to fight her tears. He lifts her and caries her to the bathroom off the game room, turns on the massage tub and places her in it. He sits on the floor next to her, "Gretchen, I lost it. I'm sorry."

She touches his cheek, "I'll be fine, Malcolm. I guess I'm just too much woman for you, is all."

"Yes, Woman, I believe you are."

That's some serious shit.

Gretchen does the morning shuffle from Malcolm's place to the Carriage House then to the office. She is nearly there when she realizes she has no recollection of making the trip; her mind is permanently fixed on her weekend with Malcolm. After the sexual fiasco, they agreed to let him take point on gentling her for the foreseeable future. She has absolutely no idea what taking point means but she agrees, anyway. The young attorney keeps her head down all day, and regardless of the amount of headspace Mr. Price fills she is remarkably productive. Late afternoon, she calls Researcher Randy to her office.

"Yo, you wanted to see me, Miss Mitchell?"

"Yes, close the door, please."

Randy sits in the chair across from her. She points to a section of her desk in front of the hipster dude. He leans forward and, "Holy shit, Miss Mitchell, I mean excuse my language, Miss Mitchell, but do you know what this is? It's an autographed ticket to the last game Malcolm Price ever played. After that game, his career was over. Damn sin. How did you score this?"

Gretchen laughs at Randy's enthusiasm. "I had a meeting with Mr. Price over the weekend, and I told him you are a fan."

"It's for me? Are you shittin me? Again, my apologies."

"There's a catch, Randy."

"There always is isn't there?" Randy says with a smile.

Gretchen chuckles. "Answer me this question and the ticket is yours. Do you know what 'taking point' means?"

Randy 'aw shucks' Miss Mitchell. "Taking point refers to the job of a point guard in basketball. The point guard controls the offense and sets the tempo of the game. Malcolm Price was point guard for the Spurs. The best damn point guard to ever play the game." Randy looks at Gretchen expectantly. "Is that all you need to know, Miss Mitchell?"

Gretchen nods. "The ticket is yours Randy. Keep it between us at the firm, okay?"

"Yes, ma'am. Thank you and if you ever see Mr. Price again, tell him Researcher Randy says the game isn't the same without him."

When Randy leaves her office, holding the signed ticket as though it is the rarest of gem or a nuclear bomb, a bit of wondering takes over. She swivels her chair, keystrokes 2013 San Antonio/Miami Heat series into her computer, and begins reading the near endless articles on His play, His injury, His career, and His place as an NBA legend. "Wow. Malcolm was big shit." She laughs at her reference, then gets back to reading about the player known worldwide as, 77. "How did I not know about this MAN?"

Old Estate Road
Father and Daughter Mitchell leave the office together. He follows her home and waits for her to join him at the Cottage. They have dinner and talk for an hour. It's a very enjoyable evening—until IT happens. At one point during kitchen clean up, Granger mentions Gretchen's suitor. She beams from ear to ear; she just can't help herself. "I would like to take you up on your offer to meet him, Daddy; if that is still agreeable to you."

"It is. When will this meeting take place and I presume your suitor has a name, Gretchen? Perhaps you would like to share it before the meeting."

"His name, yes, well, his name is Malcolm Price."

Granger Mitchell turns and leans back against the counter—one might describe the event as, 'Granger Mitchell turns and leans back against the counter in an attempt to keep himself upright'. One would most definitely be within the bounds of accuracy to do so.

"The Malcolm Price, the San Antonio Spurs, Malcolm Price, The player synonymous with his number, 77, Malcolm Price?" Granger stupefies.

"You know him?" she stupefies.

"I don't **know** him, Gretchen, but I certainly know of him. He's the best point guard to ever play basketball. Damn shame about his knee."

Gretchen falls back onto the chair she'd been upon during dinner. Her current state suggests she's in shock. "Yes, well, someone else told me that very same thing today."

"Probably Researcher Randy, he's a huge fan," Granger easily drops.

"You **know** Researcher Randy, and that he's a fan of basketball?" Gretchen stammers.

"Of course, he's an employee of mine. Really Gretchen, this relationship of yours has left you a bit daft, wouldn't you say?"

"Due respect, Daddy, but it's this conversation that has left me a bit daft, as you put it. Would you mind telling me how you know about Malcolm Price?"

"You can't be serious." And yet it appears that she is. "You didn't know who he was when you embarked on your dalliance?"

"No."

"Gretchen, that man has been a superstar pro-baller your entire young adult life; how could you not know who he is?"

"Oh, I don't know, Daddy. I was in college and law school and Europe. I studied sixty hours a week, and I work sixty hours a week. There has never been a television in this house tuned into a sport game of any type. I've never dated anyone who has ever mentioned the superstar pro-baller's name. And how on earth do you know the term pro-baller?"

Granger chuckles. "Gretchen, I'm a man of sixty-five, I've been to my fair share of games."

"Basketball games? No. You. Have. Not. Granger Mitchell at a basketball game. Honestly, I think I must have tumbled into Alice's Wonderland and there's a Mad Hatter waiting for me somewhere." She turns astonished eyes to her father and begins extricating herself from the conversation. "I need to lie down, or perhaps I am lying down and I need to wake up," she mumbles. "Do you have any time free this weekend? I'd like to have Malcolm come to the Cottage if that is acceptable." Gretchen says as she pushes herself from her chair.

"I will have Mrs. Smith give you times that will work for me, just have her put the time you choose on my calendar. I look forward to meeting your gentleman friend, Gretchen."

With that, Gretchen in Wonderland skips out the back door and into the Carriage House, thankful she came upon no white rabbits, Cheshire cats, or playing card queens along the way.

Way Too Close for Comfort

The hitman tilts the steering wheel up, slides the front seat back, and gets settled for the night. Earlier in the evening, he followed the Father and Daughter Mitchell from their law office to the gated community on Old Estate Road. The trained contract killer drove past the guard shack, "No chance of getting into that neighborhood." He did a bit of surveillance of the surrounding area, finding some access through a thickly wooded lot, but decided, "Fuck no." His plan set for the night, he went in search of a place to grab some food, and take a piss. When he returned to the posh neighborhood, all fed and drained, he pulled off the road into a heavily wooded patch, and did a bit more assessing. "The puta is a buttoned up, prissy thing. A creature of habit. She'll take the same route back to the office in the morning. I'll be right here waiting to follow along, and to cause a very unfortunate accident. Enjoy your evening, Miss Mitchell. It'll be your last."

LewPen

Four days have come and gone since Dominique's cell was inspected by CO Price — four days since she learned her parents are suing for custody of her baby — four days since the nightmares began and sent her into a downward spiral. She is completely on edge now, no longer able to live peacefully in her own little world of pretend French villas and baby strolls in the great outdoors. The prisoner hasn't played her — would you rather this or would you rather that — game of choice, and she hasn't changed her baby's name from Charlotte.

Monday is now upon her, but she angsts that she still has that night, and another full day and night before she can meet with the lawyer from Mitchell and Morgan. She lies in the fetal position on her cold hard slab and begins counting. Dominique isn't counting sheep; she's counting the people she would kill at that very moment if she had the chance... 1. Benton Brettenvue. 2. Antonio Alvarez. 3. Celia Brettenvue. 4. Rocco Fiancetti. 5. Joy Fiancetti. 6...she falls asleep.

275

Malcolm is in his living room waiting for the privacy elevator to open. The man who steps from the enclosed box is rewarded with a w.i.d.e. smile. Malcolm approaches and extends his hand in welcome then pulls his friend of thirty-years into his arms, "Damian, it's damned good to see you, come on back to the room."

"You know we live in the same zip code — we could see each other more. What's it been, two months?"

"Three, I'm a bit tied up with Mama Girl's treatments, three times a week, four hours at a whack. I just got back from one."

"How is Mama Girl?"

"She's Mama Girl. You know she's running that damned hospital now and has her nose all up in everyone's business." Malcolm laughs big.

Damian joins on in.

The men choose their places in the game room. Malcolm slides onto the leather couch he recently pressed Miss Gretchen Mitchell into and watches Damian climb aboard a gigantic leather recliner, and start pushing a bunch of buttons on the side. The grown-man-boy goes for a ride upward, downward, and side to side.

"Damn I love this thing," Damian enthuses.

"Whenever you're done, Captain. I'd like to discuss the black Escalade. Did you get anything on it?"

"Patrols haven't seen it, man. You saw it just that once?"

"I definitely saw it inch by the apartment building Friday around 7 PM, and I think it tailed me to Mama Girl's place, Saturday morning. And it was in the vicinity of Mama Girl's on Sunday. I haven't seen it since, but the tail is on Gretchen and she left here this morning," Malcolm shakes his head, "I **did not** want her going on the road alone."

A wide-ass grin takes hold of his friend's face.

"What's with the creepy smile, Captain?"

"Gretchen. She's the one," Damian states assuredly.

"The one?" Malcolm asks, though he needn't.

"The one who will bring you to your knee, man."

Malcolm's smile widens to the point of pain, "I'll be on that knee for sure. Gretchen's undone the hell out of me."

"Then we need to keep that girl safe." The men share a knowing look, and try as they might to stop IT from happening, Sage Finley suddenly fills their thoughts. They settle with them before Damian pushes on, "Tell me why Gretchen might have a tail, then we'll put together a plan. First up, does she know about the tail?"

"No."

"Who do you think is following her?"

"She's involved in the Dominique Brettenvue – Antonio Alvarez, mess. I think it has something to do with that."

"You better hope you're wrong, Malcolm. That's some serious shit."

That hideous lie.

Dominique's dreams are all over the place that night…

The Peruvian crime lord entered her bedroom. She scurried to the far wall. He smiled, "I see I am your first sexual caller. Your father said it was so, but I doubted him. American girls usually find the thrill of sex in their early teens. Your father said you are ripe and ready at seventeen. Such an honor for me to be the one to pluck and taste you, Dominique." He moved across the room, smiled at the blush on her cheeks, "A virgin's blush," he said as he ran a finger down her face and to the swell of her breasts, "it will be replaced with a woman's flush when our night together is done."

"My fa….father…" she stammered.

"Consented to this evening," he smiled. "It will be better for you to consent, as well."

~

The Peruvian crime lord entered her room. The woman got off her bed and moved to him; pressed herself against him, took hold of his erection. He smiled and ran a finger down her face and to the swell of her breasts. "There is something I want from you," he smiled. "When you consent, I will pleasure you."

"Anything," she whispered with a kiss.

"There is a man, a Federal agent, a rodent, scurrying through my organization. He must be dealt with."

She nodded, "What's your plan."

He cupped her pussy with his hand and squeezed a bit, "We use this."

~

Dominique paced the elevated balcony at Hamanasi. When the timer on her watch alerted her, she went to the bathroom and got the pregnancy test. "Shit." She started counting – backwards. "Three weeks, no four weeks. Shit. Shit. Shit." She tossed the pissed-upon stick into the trash, grabbed her things, tossed them over the balcony railing onto the ground, then climbed down the attached rope ladder, and rushed to the airport.

~

"I think we have things to discuss, Dominique."

Surprise then upset flashed and settled on her face. "You shouldn't…"

"No, Dominique, you shouldn't. He took her hand, "Look, I have business to attend to, and I won't be able to see you, or really even talk to you, much."

She rolled her eyes.

"I'm not fuckin' around here, Dominique. I want to know what your intentions are about the baby."

"I have no intentions. All I know is that I'm not going back to Paris. To be perfectly honest, Manuel, I haven't decided where to put roots yet."

"My father has a place. I could recommend you for a job. He has an Athletic Center. He will hire you and when I finish what I'm working on, I'll head up to be with you."

She smiled and placed her hand on her belly. "Okay."

"Okay?"

She smiled *that* smile. "Okay."

~

Manuel flipped Dominique onto her back, straddled her, and pinned her arms to the floor. "Dominique, what the fuck? He was going to shoot John!"

"On my orders!" Dominique hissed.

Manuel stared at the enraged, hissing woman as reality pummeled his insides. "*You* are with The Realm? *You* betrayed the Fiancettis?" Manuel screamed in Dominique's face.

Dominique spat at him. "I loathe the Fiancettis. I cringe every time a Fiancetti touches me."

Manuel lowered his head. "The baby?" he groaned.

Dominique laughed at him. "You will never see this baby. You won't live long enough to do so."

Joy Fiancetti moved to Manuel and secured Dominique's flailing legs. She bent one at an awkward angle. Dominique winced in pain. Joy yelled at the secured combatant, "Tell Manuel. Tell him the truth before I break your leg in two." Joy bent Dominique's leg farther.

Dominique cried out in pain. "This baby is not yours, Manuel. It is not a Fiancetti…"

That hideous lie banged in her head all night long.

Don't leave her alone.

Granger spends his morning puttering about the Cottage. He had an early call from Faye who is out of town for a couple days visiting her elderly mother in Trenton, New Jersey. He misses her. Warm thoughts of their anniversary weekend settle him some, but he is eager for her return on Wednesday. Truth be told, he is eager for other things—a more permanent thing with Faye. "Not sure, though. Faye has never once asked for more than what we have. And. Then. There's. Gretchen. There will be some dustup from that one." He laughs. The slam of Gretchen's back door pulls him from his thoughts. He grabs his briefcase, closes his front door behind him, slides into his car, and waits until she pulls from her driveway and passes his. She waves. He waves. He pulls out behind her as thoughts of the previous night taking hold. He shakes his head, "Wait until I tell Faye that I raised someone who didn't know who The Malcolm Price was," he laughs as he follows White Diamond through the security gate.

Still Too Close for Comfort
Antonio Alvarez's goon is pissed. He bangs his hands angrily against the steering wheel and spits his words. "That damned father is tailing his

daughter to work. What the fuck? Does the old man think she has a tail?" The goon watches for a reaction from Granger Mitchell as he moves his car alongside the old man. Takes a look into the lawyer's navy blue, Buick Regal, pulls back a bit, then moves forward for another look. "Nothing. The old fuck didn't even glance my way. He doesn't know, doesn't even suspect that she's got a tail. Just shit fucking timing." The hitman eases back a bit. "The hit needs to look like an accident." He pulls completely away from his target. "Don't tip them off," he warns himself. "Fucking puta. Your daddy can't save you much longer," he seethes as he exits the highway. "See you at the office."

Mitchell and Morgan

Gretchen flops onto her chair and immediately puts her head onto her desk. She is beyond exhausted even though she fell into the sleep of the dead the instant her head hit the pillow the night before. She laments that she slept through Malcolm's call that came in at 9 PM. She would have returned his call this morning, but he was already at the penitentiary before she woke. The woman misses the man—really misses him—to the point that she aches to see him. A wonderful, albeit unsettling occurrence. She is pulled from her thoughts by the sound of a knock on her door. She lifts her head and opens her eyes. Her paralegal is standing at the entrance to her office with several files in hand and noted concern written on his face.

"Is everything okay, Miss Mitchell?"

"Yes, yes, fine. Everything is fine. I'm afraid I didn't get enough sleep last night, that's all."

He nods, "You wanted to go over the Dominique Brettenvue file before you head to the penitentiary, tomorrow. I can come back later if you'd like."

"Right, that's right. No. No. Come on in Brett, let's get this done." Gretchen encourages.

"How about I grab us some coffees, first?" he says as he makes his way back out of Gretchen's office. On his return with the brews, the paralegal stops at his desk to answer a call, "One moment, I'll see if she is available." Brett calls out to Gretchen, "There's a Mr. Price on line one; he says it's about the Dominique Brettenvue case."

"Put the call through, and please shut my door. Good morning, Mr. Price, what can I do for you?"

"Woman, you can tell your assistant that you are available to me and only me," he teases. "I checked my milk carton this morning, and was just about to put a missing person's poster up; where were you last night?" The question isn't one he'd normally ask – but he's on edge about the black Escalade.

"I was with Alice in Wonderland," Gretchen muses.

"I feel a story coming on. I want to see you, Gretchen. You've undone me a bit."

"I could come down tonight if you'd like," Gretchen hopefully offers.

"Damn, Woman, I more than like, but only if it's early."

"I'm good here. I can skip out around three and be there by six, depending on traffic."

"Six." Malcolm disconnects.

The lawyer packs two expandable folders with Brettenvue/BOP-PA-555925 labeled client files, adds some case law Brett pulled, a legal pad and array of pens into her briefcase, and heads to Diamond White a few minutes after 3 PM. She is greeted by iffy-blue-gray skies, so she dons her shades, but leaves the convertible closed. She opens the car windows to let the air blow through her hair, and cranks *You Don't Own Me* by Grace and G-Eazy. She belts out a few lines, then purrs, "Oh, Mr. Price, I think you might own my heart—and a few other parts that respond favorably to your gentling," she laughs freely at her admission.

The goon pulls out behind Diamond White as it exits the Mitchell and Morgan parking garage. Once Gretchen hops onto I-476N, he knows she's heading to Malcolm Price's place. He pulls back and waits for the opportunity to present itself. On the second leg of the journey, at I-80W, the would-be-killer and would-be-victim hit bottleneck traffic. The goon is several cars behind her with no way to get near, no way to run her off the highway, and no way to control his rage, "Fuckin puta. Fuckin, fuckin puta," he slams his hand hard on the dashboard, and starts edging into already crowded lanes. After several failed attempts, the goon is forced to stop his aggression by some really pissed off drivers. A cacophony of horns cause Gretchen and others to check rearview mirrors to find out what the ruckus is about. He pushes low into his seat, "Fuckin puta. You might make it to Lewisburg alive, but that will be your final destination."

Hufnagle Park

Malcolm is on a bench across from his apartment waiting for Gretchen. It's 7:15, and he's worked himself up a bit with worry. When he sees Diamond White head toward him, he pushes the garage door opener and gets up to cross the street. He steps off the curb just as the black Escalade inches by. He checks the license plate – manages to get the last two digits – 88. Malcolm sprints across the street and sneaks under the door before it closes. His woman is getting out of her car as he approaches. "I was worried, Woman. Come, here, let me love you a bit." Malcolm opens his arms wide and scoops Gretchen in.

When they get to the penthouse, he excuses himself to make a call. Gretchen heads to his bedroom to store her gear then goes to the game room to wait for him. She moseys around looking at his basketball paraphernalia. She recognizes the framed number 77 team jersey as his. She is surprised it is wrinkled behind the glass of the frame. She moves on and impresses at the Championship Team photos at the White House with President George W. Bush, and at a picture of Malcolm playing a pick-up game at the White House with President Barack Obama. She marvels at the action play shots of Malcolm—his intensity, his prowess, the power of his movement caught live then memorialized in still images. She has her hand raised to a framed picture she'd recently seen online, the one that captures Malcolm's career ending injury.

"Gretchen."

She turns at the sound of his voice then turns back to the picture. "That's it, isn't it? When you hurt your knee, this picture captures that second. Right?"

Malcolm joins her and pulls her back against him. "Yes."

"Why did you hang it? Doesn't it bother you seeing it?"

"It doesn't bother me anymore. I made peace with all that years ago. It looks like it bothers you, though. What's going on, Gretchen?"

"I read about you, online. You were big shit."

Malcolm laughs big. "I like to think I'm still big shit, Woman." He takes her hand and leads her to the leather couch. "Talk to me."

"You were point guard for the Spurs," Gretchen offers.

Malcolm nods once.

"The point guard controls the offense and sets the tempo of the game."

Malcolm nods and smiles.

"So when you said you wanted to take point in our sexual trysts, what you meant is that you want to control what we do and the tempo of how we do it, right?"

Malcolm pulls her on top of him. "Woman, is this talk going to end soon because I want to take point right now and gentle you a bit."

Gretchen kisses her man. "Can we shower first?"

As soon as the warm spray finds them, he takes control and sets the tempo.

A midnight call wakes the lovers. Malcolm reads the name on his cell – leaves his bed and his woman. "Better be important, Damian."

"Turn on MSNBC."

Malcolm hightails it to the game room, turns on the tube, just in time for Breaking News...

The recent suicide of Attorney, Stuart Howard, of Denver, Colorado, seemed like a tragic ending to the life of a young lawyer. MSNBC has learned that Attorney Howard had been assigned to the case of notorious crime lord, Antonio Alvarez, currently being held at the ADX Supermax Penitentiary in Florence, Colorado. According to Attorney Howard's, widow, Cynthia Warren, her husband tried desperately to end his forced representation of Antonio Alvarez...

"Damian, talk to me," urgency deep in Malcolm's voice.

"Is Gretchen still with you?"

"Yes. Why?"

"Malcolm, that girl cannot be left alone until I've had some time to work this. I've got a call into the Denver PD saying I need some background. I should hear something tomorrow. What is Gretchen doing tomorrow?"

"She's going to the penitentiary to meet with Dominique Brettenvue, then home."

"Don't leave her alone," Damian warns.

Malcolm feels Gretchen's presence, he turns to see her standing in the doorway, sleep and confusion in her eyes. "I've got to go Damien. Gretchen is here." Before Malcolm can turn the television off, MSNBC starts the breaking news report, again. Malcom goes to her. "Gretchen, I want you off the Brettenvue case. After tomorrow, you need to get this case assigned to someone else," he says firmly.

"Because some lawyer in Colorado killed himself?"

"No, because someone has been tailing you for the last few days."

"What are you talking about?"

"A black Escalade followed you to my place Friday night, then I saw it again on Saturday, and again when we were are Mama Girl's, and again tonight when you pulled into the garage. Captain Johnson of the Lewisburg Police Department has been checking into it for me. He's the one who called about the news report on Alvarez. He's going to check a few things out tomorrow, and until then you aren't going to be out of my sight. In fact, get to bed, you're coming with me to LewPen in the morning. We leave at 6:30."

Gretchen crawls into Malcolm's bed and into a banging nightmare…

She pulled Diamond White onto the highway. A chill ran her spine when she realized the road was bumper to bumper full of black vehicles — black Escalades. She looked at the car to her right and to her left. The windows were tinted, leaving no way of knowing who was driving. The forward crawl of cars slowed, then stopped. Diamond White was boxed in by black Escalades. One by one doors opened...

Her laugh turns to screams.

The exhausted woman drags herself to the kitchen for a cup of coffee. Malcolm eyes her and teases, "Not a morning person?"

"I do not understand why I have to go with you so early in the morning. It is morning, right?" He hands her a cup, she takes a sip, her brain starts functioning. Sort of. "I made a bumper to bumper, four-hour trip by myself yesterday, I'm rather sure I can make a twenty-minute trip this morning," she hisses a yawn, and realizes Malcolm is staring at her feet. She looks down, "Why are you looking at the floor, Malcolm?"

"Watching your foot stomping, Woman. You do that when you're mad. Get your things, we're leaving."

"You know, Malcolm, I don't think I'm enjoying this demanding side of you."

"You seem to be enjoying the other sides of me; I think you'll handle this one. Let's go."

By the time they reach the garage level, Gretchen has introduced Malcolm to her demanding side. She insists she drive her own car with him following. "…that way, if we receive the all-clear from Captain Johnson, I can head back to Philly straight from the penitentiary," she presents her closing argument with a flip of her platinum hair and an, 'I'm not budging' stare of her cornflower blues. Her little snit has garnered a few stares from other residents at 275 who are also heading out.

Malcolm consents, "I'll follow you."

The hitman waits until the white Mercedes and the black Land Rover leave the parking garage before pulling his replacement gray BMW SUV into traffic. "Yeah, you made me last night in the black Escalade, Price, not this morning, though." The goon doesn't need to follow them, he knows where they are going, so he stays way back. "There's nothing I can do to stop you from meeting with Dominique Brettenvue this morning, Attorney Mitchell, but I can keep you from reporting back to your boss-daddy this afternoon."

LewPen

Dominique sits on the concrete slab waiting for an escort to bring her to her 10 AM meeting with Gretchen Mitchell. She doesn't have a clock or other time piece in her cell, but she knows the sounds of prison life, and she knows that it is well past ten. A tiny panic begins in the pit of her stomach. "What if the lawyer doesn't come? What if it's too late and the Brettenvue's already gained custody? What if I never get to tell Manuel Xavier that Charlotte is his child?"

Gretchen has been sitting in the locked meeting room since 7 AM. She has spent nearly all of that time alone. She's paced, she's tapped her fingers on the table, she's knocked on the locked door, she's sworn—on several occasions—and at several decibels.

When CO Price opens the door, she almost rams him. "Where have you been? Why am I still waiting? Where the hell is Dominique? What is going on?"

Malcolm laughs. "Quiet down, Woman, and I'll answer your questions. I have been working. You are still waiting because the prisoner isn't ready for the visit. She went to the infirmary this morning. I believe that answers your first set of questions. Do you have others, Counselor?"

"Is something wrong with the baby? Will she be able to meet with me? Would you like to do a little sex play while we wait?" Gretchen winks and smiles.

"There is nothing wrong with the baby. She will meet with you shortly. Sex play with you, Counselor, anytime, anyplace." Malcolm steps toward her then stops when there is a knock at the door. He unlocks it and speaks with a CO in the hall. He comes back inside, closes the door behind him. "Dominique will be here after lunch at 1:30. Come on, I'll take you to the commissary. Leave your stuff here, the room will be locked."

Mitchell and Morgan
Faye Smith is late getting to the office from her trip back from New Jersey. Traffic from Trenton to Philadelphia was backed up for miles due to an overturned diesel fuel truck, and by the time she enters Granger's office it is after 1 PM. Granger pulls her into his arms and holds her close, "I missed you, Faye. I'm very pleased you are home."

The longtime lovers and friends spend nearly an hour catching up. Mostly, it is Granger filling Faye in on Gretchen's suitor, Malcolm Price. Faye nearly pees her pants from a fit of laughter when Granger tells her, "Gretchen had absolutely no idea who Malcolm Price was when she began seeing him. My daughter became quite indignant at the notion that I know anything about basketball, let alone anything about the superstar point guard for the San Antonio Spurs."

Faye is still laughing when she begins opening the pile of mail addressed to Granger Mitchell. Her laugh turns to screams when she opens the letter from Attorney Stuart Howard of Denver, Colorado…

Mr. Mitchell,
My name is Stuart Howard. I am a court-appointed attorney for Antonio Alvarez. While there are countless criminal charges pending against my client, his sole focus is gaining

possession of the unborn child of Dominique Brettenvue. Mr. Alvarez has a very good chance of succeeding. He has someone inside the Child Protective Services in Pennsylvania, and he has leverage against Benton Brettenvue should he and his wife gain custody through the Philadelphia courts. Alvarez has assured me that his child will be given to his family in Peru, through one of these means.

During a recent visit to the ADX Supermax Penitentiary in Florence, Colorado, Antonio Alvarez ordered me to arrange a "don't stop" contract killing on your daughter, Gretchen Mitchell. The phone number I called to arrange the hit is 305-555-1324. There is no defense of my actions, however, I was assured by Alvarez that if I did not place the call by the end of business that day, I would find my wife and children dead when I returned home. I placed the call so I could save my family. I am writing this letter so you can save yours.

My soul is damned for all eternity, and I am truly sorry,
Stuart Howard

LewPen

Gretchen and Malcolm wait inside the lawyer meeting room for Dominique. The attorney is antsy from being locked up all day. She paces the tiny room, stops on a dime when a knock comes.

Malcolm unlocks the door and steps aside. The escort CO ushers Dominique Brettenvue into the room, seats the prisoner, works her chains through bolts on the floor, introduces the prisoner by her prison number, "BOP-PA-555925," hands paperwork to CO Price, and says "Thirty minutes," before leaving.

Gretchen is surprised by Dominique's appearance. She's seen her on news reports for months, and has a vague recollection of meeting her at the Brettenvue family home once, but still, the woman before her looks more like a grade school teacher than a criminal mastermind. The lawyer puts Dominique's features to memory; *pretty in a very natural way, strawberry-blonde hair that softly curls from end to end, pale green eyes, and a smattering of freckles across the bridge of her nose, which is slightly turned up at the end.* Gretchen suddenly realizes that while she is sizing up Dominique, she, too, is being sized up.

"I met you once at the Brettenvue's," Dominique begins.

Gretchen nods. "You were probably in high school."

"I was seventeen. That's the year Benton Brettenvue pimped me out to Antonio Alvarez." Dominique watches Gretchen for a reaction. There is none.

Gretchen pulls a breath, "Sadly, Dominique, that does not surprise me about your father."

"You don't like Benton Brettenvue. Why are you representing him and Celia in this Petition for Custody?"

"My personal feelings for Benton and Celia Brettenvue are irrelevant. I am here to inform you of their interests and intended actions to obtain custody of your child."

"My daughter. My baby is a girl," Dominique says to a reward of kicks and skirmishes by the baby in discussion. "She's been very active today."

"Is that the reason for the delay in our meeting this morning?" Gretchen catches movement coming from Malcolm's direction.

"No. I'm not sure why there was a delay," Dominique answers dismissively.

Gretchen eyes Malcolm who avoids her look.

The prisoner interrupts the moment. "Attorney Mitchell, does your father, the almighty Granger Mitchell, know of your duplicity in this matter?"

"He does not."

"And when he finds out?"

"Our firm will be forced to end representation of the Brettenvues. That is why I suggest we conduct our business and put an end to your parent's ability to lay claim to your daughter." Gretchen pulls a legal pad and pen from her briefcase. "Dominique, do you have just cause why your parents should not be considered as guardians or as adoptive parents to…" Gretchen stops and looks at Dominique. "Have you named your daughter? If you have, I would like to address her by her name."

"Charlotte. You may call her Charly, as well," Dominique says with pride.

"Charly, very sweet. Okay, Dominique do you have any reasons why Benton and Celia Brettenvue are unfit to raise Charly?"

Dominique breaks into a fit of laughter. "I have a million reasons why they should be locked in this Federal penitentiary with me, and I am happy to share them with you, but I have a better way of keeping Charly away from them."

Gretchen puts her pen down and leans back in her chair. "Care to share your plan?"

"I want Charly's father to adopt her."

Air catches in Gretchen's throat. "You want Antonio Alvarez to adopt your baby?" she asks incredulously.

"Of course not. Antonio Alvarez is not Charlotte's father. Manuel Xavier is my baby's father."

Gretchen spends the remainder of their meeting learning who Manuel Xavier is and listening to the events that unfolded at the Fiancetti Compound the day Dominique was captured. "Do you have any proof of paternity that names Manuel Xavier as Charly's father?"

Dominique nods. "There is proof hidden in the guard shack where I used to bunk when I worked for Rocco Fiancetti."

"Why did you lie to Mr. Xavier about the paternity?"

"Because I hate Manuel, but having my daughter with him is better than having her with anyone else involved in this mess. Most specifically, the Brettenvues."

Precisely one half-hour later, prisoner BOP-PA-555925 is prepared for her escort back to her cell. Before Dominique leaves, Gretchen asks a final question, "When was the last time you were seen in the infirmary?"

Dominique thinks a moment. "Time is difficult to track in here, but it was probably two weeks ago, why?"

"Just making sure you and Charlotte are being cared for."

The second Dominique leaves, Malcolm moves to Gretchen to explain. She raises her hand. "Don't. As soon as I gather my things, I am out of here. I will see you at your place. We need to talk."

"Gretchen, don't leave. Wait until my shift ends. Please."

Gretchen hasn't looked at him once. She shoves her files and notes in her briefcase and walks to the door. "Open it. Now, Malcolm."

He steps toward her. She steps away. Reluctantly, the CO unlocks, and opens the door. He leads her to the security desk in silence. He hands her a visitation form for the following week then her belongings—holding the last of them a bit longer than necessary. "Gretchen, please."

The *very* pissed off woman takes her things and leaves him. He watches her get into Diamond White and drive away.

Then he watches a gray BMW SUV
follow her out of the parking lot.

This wasn't an accident.

Gretchen's tires squeal as she speeds away from LewPen. She seethes while she scolds the nothingness around her. "I wasted a whole damn day sitting in that meeting room— and **you** planned it, manipulated it, with deceit, I might add." Tears sting her eyes, but hold still for a minute before streaming down her face. "You're all…'let's get to know one another'…well know this, Mr. Malcolm Price, I don't take kindly to being lied to." A nudge from some place deep tries to move her toward a defense of the man. "No! He shouldn't have. He didn't need to. I would have stayed had he asked me." A new round of tears fall, "No. I wouldn't have. Even if I needed to. Still he should have asked me." The wounded woman can't go deep enough to really reason her way through the emotional shitstorm. The pain she's dealing with is right on the surface, so she stays there with it. Cries through it.

She roars into the underground garage at 275 having no recollection of making the trip or making notice of the gray BMW SUV on her tail. She pulls Diamond White into her designated spot, barely registers the BMW as it drives past her and takes a left at the end of the garage. She gathers her things from her seat, glances at her cell before she drops it into her briefcase,

"Twenty missed calls, what the hell?" With a sense of urgency she slams the car door and moves quickly toward the privacy elevator. She hasn't made it past the trunk of Diamond White when she hears the rev of an engine and the squeal of tires. She turns her head from side to side and finds the source of the noise, the gray BMW she saw pass her when she pulled into the garage.

She halts her forward movement when the vehicle rounds the corner. She jumps back and throws herself against a parked car on her right just as the BMW guns it and smashes into Diamond White. She pulls herself upright and starts toward the BMW. "What the hell!" she screams before reality takes hold. *This wasn't an accident.* She turns and takes one step toward the elevator, just as the driver jams into reverse and squeals back toward her. She darts back toward the parked car, scurries around the backend a fraction of a second before the BMW rams into it pushing it hard against her legs. The terrified woman rights herself and bolts toward the elevator. The BMW speeds the length of the parking lot and whips around the corner at the far end.

Gretchen reaches the elevator, bangs Malcolm's security code into the keypad with shaking fingers. She bounces from foot to foot, urging the doors to open, "Come on. Open. Open. Open!" She bangs the buttons with the palm of her hand, "Come on. Come on!" She throws herself inside the protective box, bangs the up button, and watches the door close just as the driver makes the corner, and speeds toward the elevator. Gretchen bangs back against the wall, her heart nearly pounding out of her chest, her rapid breaths catching painfully inside. When the elevator door opens into the penthouse apartment, she collapses onto the floor. She doesn't do anything but shake and dry heave until she hears the call for the elevator. The terrified and injured woman drags herself across the room, and tucks herself into an empty area next to the sideboard. She struggles to slow her ragged breaths – exhales fully and loudly when she hears Malcolm calling her name.

"Gretchen!"

She peeks from around the furniture, then winces in pain when he pulls her into his arms.

"Gretchen! What the hell? Diamond White is smashed to fuck, and your briefcase and files are all over the floor."

Gretchen wants to tell him what happened, but she can't stop sobbing or shaking.

Malcolm carries her to his bedroom, puts her onto his lap, and covers them with a blanket. He holds her until her racking sobs slow and her shaking ebbs toward occasional spasms. "The police are downstairs. You're safe now. Captain

Johnson, will be up soon. Gretchen, I need to take a look at you. Woman, please let me look at you."

The ping of the elevator, announces the captain's arrival. "Damian, back here."

Gretchen is full-on shaking when Captain Johnson approaches. She squints her eyes and leans forward a bit, "Jet Johnson?" she asks through shivers.

Malcom leans her away from his chest and drills her with a stare. "You know who Jet Johnson is, a two-bit college athlete, but you didn't know who I was?"

"Hey!" Jet snaps, "I was a track and field phenom, and well on my way to the Olympics. Show some respect." The captain leans close and examines the woman clinging to his best friend, "I think she's in shock," he opines.

Malcolm exhales loudly, "She'd have to be in shock to know who you are."

The traumatized woman's tears return. Malcolm adjusts her on his lap, causing her to wince in pain. "Gretchen, I need to check you for injuries. I'm going to lie you down and look, okay?" He helps her roll off him and sits on the edge of the bed. He checks her right side because she is clearly favoring it. He lifts the bottom of her V-neck sweater up to her bra; red welts raise from her hip to breast. Malcolm shoots Damian a look.

He walks toward the door, "I'll call Wanda."

While they are alone, Malcolm eases Gretchen out of her sweater then goes to work on her pants. The entire right side of his woman is covered in angry bruises. They travel from breast to ankle, some wrap toward her abdomen and some toward her back. Whenever Gretchen is moved, she cradles her right elbow. Malcolm covers her when Damian returns.

"Wanda is on her way. She asked if Gretchen banged her head; if so, we're supposed to keep her awake. She also asked why we didn't take her to the hospital. Actually, she said, "What in tarnation is she doing in Malcolm's bedroom and not in an emergency room?" I told her Gretchen is safer here for the time being. She agreed to come on the condition that her word is the final word. I'll tell you, man, ever since my woman became a physician's assistant, she's as bossy as all get out."

Malcolm moves his gigantic hands softly across Gretchen's head feeling for bumps. "I don't feel any raised areas, so I'll let her sleep until Wanda gets here. Stay with her, Damian, I need to call her father."

Faye Smith puts Malcolm's call directly through to Granger and joins him in his office. The lawyer takes control. "Mr. Price, a 'don't stop' contract has been put out on Gretchen by Antonio Alvarez. He wants my daughter dead.

Do you know where she is? I've been frantically trying to reach her."

"Mr. Mitchell, Gretchen is with me. There was an attempt made on her life this afternoon. Someone tried to run her down and in the process she's been banged up. Medical personnel are on the way to my home, but I think you should come and be with her."

"Address please."

Physician's Assistant Wanda Johnson greets her husband of fifteen years with a quick kiss then she greets her friend of fifteen years with a hug. Wanda Johnson is an itty-bit of a woman in stature, a gigantic woman of character, heart, and soul "Okay, Malcolm wake Gretchen, tell her who I am, and then the two of you get out." The bossy one leaves to wash her hands, glove up, and get her medical bag set. When she returns, the patient is awake, though groggy.

Malcolm introduces the women then he and Damian leave as they have been ordered. "Man, she's a bossy thing," Malcolm says as they walk past.

Wanda smirks then gets to work. "Gretchen, I'm Wanda, Damian's wife."

"Jet's wife," Gretchen whispers.

"Good, you remember him. Were you introduced before the accident?" Wanda asks trying to get a gauge on her patient's thought process and memory range.

"No, he's a running god," Gretchen says on a yawn.

Wanda runs her fingers all around Gretchen's head feeling for bumps then laughs at Gretchen's description of her man as a god, "I suppose he was. Were you track and field?"

Gretchen nods, "At UPenn. Jet was...before me at Penn State, but he's a PA boy so...so...UPenn loved him, too," she shivers her answers.

"Okay, Gretchen, you're doing good. I'm going to get Jet; I'll be right back". The physician's assistant doesn't have to go far. Malcolm and Damian are right outside the door. She waves them in and has them stand close enough to hear, but outside the line of sight. Wanda gently touches Gretchen's shoulder rousing her from a daydream state. She places a continual blood pressure cuff on Gretchen's arm, and takes her pulse. "Gretchen, you were about to tell me what happened in the garage. I'm going to examine you while you talk, okay?"

Gretchen nods. "I was crying...and driving, and I didn't...I didn't see a black Escalade." Gretchen yawns.

"Did you see any car?" Wanda looks into Gretchen's eyes and ears and runs her fingers down the sides of her neck and along her shoulders.

"At the garage, a gray SUV followed me in and drove around the corner." Gretchen stops talking, her eyes dark back and forth as though they are watching the events on a loop, her pulse increases, her hands start trembling, her vitals spike.

"Gretchen, I think we should talk more later. Go ahead and close your eyes for a bit." Wanda pulls back the covers and examines the bruising on Gretchen's front, side and back. After several minutes, she joins the men. "I don't think we have to worry about a concussion, and the injuries to her right side, while dramatic, do not look like they were inflicted by a moving vehicle. My guess is that she threw herself against or onto a parked car. My professional opinion is that you should take her to the ER, but I know your concerns. I'd like to hear from her how she feels before I decide."

Wanda returns to Gretchen and gently rouses her. She offers her a sip of water. "How are you feeling, Gretchen?"

"Sore."

"Any particular area that's particularly sore?"

"My elbow and my hip, I think." Gretchen yawns.

"Do you know how you injured yourself?"

"I hit a parked car. Twice."

"Why did you hit the parked car, twice?"

"He went forward, then he went backward." Gretchen's eyes fill with tears that begin flowing. "Tell Malcolm I'm sorry. I should have listened. I shouldn't have left him. I should tell him I love him."

Malcolm walks to the far side of his bed and lies down with his woman. He gently traces the contours of her face and whispers, "I love you, too, Gretchen."

May we see her?

Captain Johnson is walking his wife to her car when Granger Mitchell pulls into the garage. The captain introduces himself and takes Granger and Faye to the penthouse. Malcolm Price approaches Granger and Faye with outstretched hand. "I'm sorry these are the circumstances of our introductions. Gretchen just fell asleep, so let me explain what happened, then I'll take you to her."

"Before you begin, Malcolm," Granger gives Captain Johnson the letter from Attorney Stuart Howard. "That is evidence connected to what happened here today. We put it into a baggie, but both of our prints are on it, as are the firm's mail clerk's, perhaps others, too."

Damian and Malcolm read the letter—it confirms their suspicions and puts a whole new light on what they are dealing with.

"Mr. Mitchell, have you informed the authorities, Philly PD, the FBI, anyone about this letter?"

"No. We opened the envelope, read the letter, and immediately began calling Gretchen. We were about to contact the authorities when Malcolm called. I expect you will handle this appropriately, Captain." He turns to Malcolm. "How is Gretchen, and may we see her?"

"Physician's assistant, Wanda Johnson, just completed an examination. She has asked that Gretchen be examined and X-rayed in her office in the morning. She ruled out a concussion, thankfully, but Gretchen has extensive bruising from her chest to her ankle on her right side, and she is favoring her right elbow. It appears she threw herself onto a parked car, first when her assailant drove toward her and then when he backed his car toward her. She is sleeping, but if you would like to sit with her you may."

Granger stands from the couch and extends his hand to Faye. "May we both see her?"

"This way."

After getting Granger and Faye set in the bedroom he meets Damian in the living room. His friend hands Malcolm a series of pictures printed from the security camera footage. It shows exactly what happened to Gretchen Mitchell—and how close to death she came.

Get rid of them.

    Malcolm calls LewPen and gets the next few days off from work. He takes Gretchen to see Wanda Johnson, and after a series of X-rays and another poke and prod here and there she is sent back to the penthouse, her right arm in a sling as a reminder to favor the heavily bruised elbow. The visitors who arrived the night before are waiting at the penthouse for her return. Gretchen slept through the bedside visit of Granger and Faye, and hasn't a clue of their presence in Lewisburg. The couple thought it best to send her on her way that morning without the ensuing fuss about their overnight stay. She is back at 275—let the fuss begin!

    To say Gretchen is shocked to see her lawyer-father and his administrative assistant exit the spare bedroom suite and join her in the game room is an understatement—of gargantuan proportions. "Malcolm," she says when her eyes fall upon Mr. Granger Mitchell and Mrs. Faye Smith, "I think Wanda may have missed a concussing-type bump on my head, because I think Granger Mitchell and Faye Smith just exited the guest suite, together," she whisper finishes.

    Granger moves to the couch upon which Gretchen rests, lifts her lower legs, sits down, and places them onto his lap. "About that," her father begins, "Faye and I are together."

"Faye?" Gretchen croaks. "Mrs. Smith, you mean that Faye?" Gretchen blinks rapidly. "Granger Mitchell and Faye Smith are *together*? What does 'we are together' mean....no, no, don't tell me what that means—tell me instead what you are wearing? Are those sweatpants, and is that a long-sleeved T-shirt? Are they Malcolm's sweats and tee? And the sneakers? Are you wearing sneakers? Oh, good Lord. Where is your suit and your cufflinks? Where are your wingtips?" She stares then blinks, stares then blinks. "I believe I've gone daft as you put it, Daddy, or I've concussed myself, or I'm sleeping in Wonderland again. I mean, what woman has a hitman try to kill her by running her over, and a father who tries to kill her by inducing a stroke. What the hell is going on in my life?"

Granger looks at Faye and then at Malcolm who has taken up wall space as far from the shitshow as possible. "Well, that went better than expected," Granger says.

After a moment, Gretchen speaks. "Daddy, how long have you and Faye—I suppose I may call her that since you two are together, right?" Gretchen looks between her father and the woman in his life. "Daddy, how long have you been with Faye?"

"We celebrated our twenty-fifth anniversary this past weekend."

The stunned woman hasn't a clue if he said anything else because she fainted. When she comes to, Malcolm has her upper body on his lap, and Faye and Granger are flapping around getting a glass of water and a cold compress.

Gretchen whispers up to Malcolm, "Get rid of them. We need to talk."

Malcolm dismisses the fluttering duo. "Granger, Faye, we need a few minutes."

Once gone, Gretchen winces herself up and onto his lap. "Malcolm Price, did you tell me last night that you love me, because if that is true, it is the only thing that makes any sense to me, even though we've only known one another a handful of days, and it'd be very unusual for love to take hold of one's heart so quickly, but it has taken hold of my heart, and I should say for the record that I have no plans whatsoever to let it go, but perhaps I was dreaming when you whispered words of love, albeit it was a lovely dream, but I seem to be drifting into Alice's Wonderland quite a bit lately, so it's very possible everything is a dream, oh, Malcolm, are you a dream...no, no, don't tell me because I never want to wake from this dream and..."

Malcolm pulls his woman to him and laughs big. "I love you Gretchen Mitchell, you've undone me."

"Yes, well, I believe you've undone me too, Malcolm. Now, about them..." Her next rant is cut blunt by the single-file approach of Mr. Granger Mitchell, Mrs. Faye Smith, and Captain Damian Johnson. "Oh, good, God, what now?" she says from her perch as they enter the game room en masse.

Malcolm, reading the intensity in his friend's face, moves from under Gretchen and crosses the room. As he passes Damian, he receives a shake of the head — the one that signals shit is happening.

Damian takes point. "You and I are going to have a serious conversation, Gretchen. You are going to keep still until I've said my piece, and then I will answer your questions."

"Geez, Jet, no, how are you today, Gretchen?" she asks playfully.

"No." Damian hands Attorney Stuart Howard's letter to the injured attorney and waits until she reads it. He knows she is finished because her face has lost whatever color she had and she begins trembling.

"Okay, I see you've grasped the seriousness of the situation you're in."

Gretchen nods. She wants to look at Malcolm, but Damian is all in her face blocking her view.

"I've spoken with members of the Denver Police Department, who referred me to a Special Agent with the Colorado FBI field office who referred me to the Director of FICA, whose division is the lead investigative body handling

The Realm's crimes. The only reason—I want to impress upon you that the **only** reason—I am being included in any of their conversations is because I am in possession of that letter, and I am the official providing protective custody of you. All that changes as soon as the Feds get here this afternoon."

The Captain checks Gretchen for signs of life, "You still with me?"

She nods. Sort of.

"Good. Before the FBI gets here, you need to understand the following things: 1) Antonio Alvarez, a Peruvian crime lord put a 'don't stop' contract out on you which means his hitman will continue his efforts to kill you until he succeeds – 2) this hit **may** be about the baby Dominique Brettenvue is carrying, but we need to remember that both of these criminals are behind bars because of their association with The Realm – 3) Attorney Stuart Howard arranged that hit to keep Alvarez from killing the attorney's wife and two young children – 4) you are now a material witness against Antonio Alvarez for his murder attempt against you, which is only part of the charges that will be brought against him based on Attorney Howard's letter – 5) the FBI wants you in protective custody, **with them** – 6) you will be leaving with them unless you can lawyer yourself out of this situation – 7) how are you doing today, Gretchen?" He takes her hand in his and gives it a squeeze.

She smiles wide and squeezes back. "I am much better, thank you for asking, Jet." She leans around the captain, and finds her father standing near Malcolm, "Daddy, please pull whatever strings you need to pull to keep me here with Malcolm."

Granger nods, "I'll call Stacy." He leaves the room with Faye.

"Malcolm, I should have asked you if you even want me to stay. Apparently, I bring danger to your doorstep, I can leave if you'd prefer," Gretchen says worriedly.

"Woman, you are never leaving me again. Let's work with Damian and make a plan to keep you safe." He smiles and winks.

Name it.

Stacy Remington, the newly appointed Director of FICA, is an accomplished woman. She graduated Harvard Law, and attended both the John F. Kennedy School of Government, and Massachusetts Institute of technology. The surefooted young woman thumped from the world of academia, grabbed hold of the first rung of the professional ladder at FICA—And. Started Climbing. It should be noted that Stacy Remington can trace her auspicious ascension to a single step she took when she was in junior high school…

Attorney Granger Mitchell accepted an invitation to visit three Harlem public schools after winning a landmark lawsuit that had been dubbed, Mitchell v The Man by inner city youth. Granger and his then partner, Fitz Morgan, championed a case against mega corporations that slapped playgrounds and ballfields on toxic landfills in blighted neighborhoods. The "recreational space" wasn't all fun and games when it was learned that the play areas exposed kids to cancer-causing agents, and sent many to early graves. The celebrated attorney could have done any number of things after his mammoth win—hit the morning news circuit, sit with interviewers at *Time*, or *Newsweek*, or travel the country on paid speaking gigs. None of those things were of interest to Granger Mitchell. He spent his fifteen minutes of fame doing what **he** wanted—delivering an inspirational, "**You** can do anything **You** want to do," speech at select schools. After a well-attended, and well-received lecture, he was walking toward the exit door at PS-55, when a tenacious Stacy Remington stepped from her patrol line and snuck next to the famed attorney. As bold as all get out, she tugged on the man's sleeve.

"I want to be you when I grow up."

The larger-than-life-man reached into his breast pocket, pulled out his business card, handed it to Stacy and said, "Write me a letter about yourself, I will write back."

No one there that day thought either one would write those letters—except for Stacy and Granger, that is. She wrote her letter. He wrote his letter. Then they wrote dozens more over the years; Stacy listing her accomplishments and her struggles, Granger mentoring and encouraging her when she questioned whether she'd ever really get out of Harlem.

"You get the grades, the rest will take care of itself," he said during a birthday phone call one year. The celebratory call was from Stacy to Granger.

~

Stacy Remington got the grades and was accepted to every undergraduate college and university to which she applied. She chose the College of William & Mary for her undergraduate work.

"Why William & Mary," Granger asked the beaming high school graduate.

"It is one of the original nine Colonial colleges, and it would have beaten Harvard as the first chartered school of higher education in America had it not been for the 'Indian uprising' of 1622. I figure the first Remington to leave Harlem for advanced learning ought to do that learning at a historical place as fine as Williamsburg." She leaned in and whispered into Granger's ear, "Besides, if William & Mary was good enough for Presidents Thomas Jefferson, James Monroe, and John Tyler, it is good enough for Stacy Remington."

Granger laughed big at his spunky little friend and added, "Don't forget George Washington, he got his…"

"Surveyor's license from W&M," Stacy finished her mentor's sentence. "You ain't telling me something I don't already know, Mr. Granger."

He laughed again, "No, I suppose I'm not, Miss Stacy."

That bit of history is why Stacy Remington, FICA Director at the FBI takes Granger Mitchell's call that morning. "Granger, I was going to call you about Gretchen, how is she doing?"

"She is resting and pulling herself together, thank you. I need a favor, Stacy."

"Name it."

Granger returns to the game room and gives a thumbs up which sets Gretchen off on another one of her 'what the hell is going on' word mashes. "Did Granger Mitchell give us a thumbs up? And if so, does that thumbs up indicate success in his endeavor, or is that thumbs up some sort of elitist gesture of which I am unaware? Seriously, Daddy, who are you? I left the office two days ago thinking Granger Mitchell is a buttoned-up, upper crust, tightly wound, attorney-father—and today, said attorney-father is prancing around in sweatpants with his 'woman' of twenty-five years superglued to his hip, whilst giving thumbs up gestures when he enters the game room of a former basketball player who said attorney-father refers to as a b-baller. I think I may be experiencing a break from reality."

Granger waits until his sputtering daughter stops for a breath. "If you are quite finished, Gretchen, the thumbs up indicates success in my endeavor. FICA Director Remington will inform the field agents that you are to stay here under the protection of Captain Damian

Johnson with the aid of the Federal government as the Captain sees fit."

Damian gets to his feet. "I have some work to do."

"Bye, Jet," Gretchen playfully calls from the couch.

"Bye, Gretchen." Damian smiles wide as he walks past his best friend, "Don't tell Wanda, but I think I love your woman."

"Way ahead of you, Jet."

After the law enforcer leaves to do law enforcing things, Malcolm gets a call from Wanda Johnson checking on Gretchen, and informing, "...and I took Mama Girl to her dialysis appointment and filled her in on the happenings at 275."

"Two bossy women descending upon that hospital. Hardly seems right," Malcolm teases. He's just about to tell Gretchen that Wanda expects calm and relaxation from the patient when he watches her get off the buttery-soft leather couch. "Gotta go, Wanda. The woman is on the move."

Gretchen takes center-floor. "I'd like the three sweatpants-wearing people in this room to join me in the living room. Malcolm, have you any idea where my scattered belongings ended up after being strewn about the garage?" she calls from over her shoulder.

He was going to tell her to sit back down and rest, instead he falls in line. As the others head to the living room, he grabs the unassembled mess from a kitchen counter and puts them onto the coffee table in front of Gretchen – then does a bit of grousing, "Bossy women coming out of the woodwork, I tell you."

Gretchen smiles wide at her man then turns her attention to Faye. "These two men are going to have certain reactions to what I am going to say. I would appreciate a little female backup."

Faye nods, eyes Granger and shrugs. "It's a woman thing," she says in a preemptive defense.

"Yes, Faye, a determined woman's thing," Gretchen smiles. "I will stay in protective custody without complaint and I will cease visiting Dominique Brettenvue at the penitentiary, IF certain conditions are met." There is a dip of her employer's head indicating his willingness to listen, and a shake of her man's head indicating his preemptive disapproval. Gretchen laughs, "Malcolm, you don't even know what I'm about to say."

"I know I'm not gonna like it."

"Perhaps not," she continues with a laugh, "I stay on this case, but I think we should do whatever possible to keep Dominique's unborn baby from the clutches of Benton and Celia Brettenvue."

The senior partner of Mitchell and Morgan starts to say something—his much junior associate interrupts him. "I know certain things about Dominique's baby that will render any and all custody proceedings you might mount on behalf of the Brettenvues moot. More to the point, Daddy, you should not be representing the likes of Celia and Benton Brettenvue."

Malcolm who is standing across the room with his back pressed tight to the brick wall and his feet crossed at the ankles, shifts his posture in expectation of a Granger Mitchell outburst. What he gets—what Gretchen gets—is another shocker.

"I agree," Granger says.

"I do too," Faye says.

"I'll be damned," Malcolm says.

"What the unholy hell is going on in my life?" Gretchen asks.

Oh, for Heaven's sake.

Researcher Randy bounds to the eighth floor after being summoned to the inner sanctum. He stops cold at the sound of Granger Mitchell's voice amplified through a desktop intercom, "Send Randall in when he gets here, Mrs. Smith."

"Yo! The great and powerful boss has spoken."

Faye stifles a laugh and follows the hipster into the office.

"Have a seat Randy. I have an assignment for you. It is outside the purview of your functions at the firm, but the request for your assistance comes from Miss Mitchell."

Randy nods.

"Gretchen will be working remotely for the foreseeable future. There will be a need to transport supplies and files to and from this office to her location. She has asked that you be responsible for this service. You will be working exclusively for her here at this office and where she is currently located. All other work of yours will be reallocated. Before I give you further details, are you interested in this assignment?"

"Yes, sir."

"Very well." Granger gets up from his desk and takes the seat next to Randy. "There was an attempt made on Gretchen's life and she is currently in protective custody." Granger pauses so Randy can process that news.

"Excuse me sir, is Miss Mitchell hurt? I really hope you say no, sir."

"She has sustained injuries, but she is mending. There is a current threat out on her life. When you leave this office, you cannot, and you will not say a single word to a single soul about this situation. The only two people in this office complex who know anything about this situation are in this room with you. If word gets out, you will be terminated, immediately. Is that understood?"

"Yes, sir. You can count on Researcher Randy, sir."

"That's what Gretchen said. I am going to give you an address. It is for a building in Lewisburg, a residential building where Gretchen is staying. When you leave this office, you will take the box that's sitting on my desk to that address. There will be Federal agents who will frisk you and escort you to Gretchen. From that point, she will direct your services. Do you have any issues or questions?"

"My wheels aren't the greatest."

Granger nods to Faye who leaves the room. "There will be a car downstairs within minutes. Do you need to return to your office for anything?"

"No, sir."

"Very well. Thank you for agreeing to this." Granger extends his hand and Researcher Randy shakes it.

After Randy leaves for Lewisburg, Faye returns to Granger. "He's going to pass out when he sees Malcolm Price."

"That's what Gretchen said." The couple enjoy a laugh.

275 Market Street

Researcher Randy steps from the privacy elevator, smiles wide when he sees Gretchen sitting upright. He walks past the FBI agent who's standing just inside the penthouse apartment. "**Not** consenting to another round of 'stop and frisk,' dude."

The agent scowls.

Gretchen laughs then waves her unslung arm toward Randy, "Just put the box on the coffee table. I wouldn't want you to drop it."

"Pish, it's not that heavy, Miss Mitchell."

"Still, you might drop it," she smiles then calls out, "Darling, we have company."

When Researcher Randy sees 6'5" NBA Champion Malcolm Price walk into the room he nods at his boss, "Damned straight, Miss Mitchell, I would have dropped that box." The FAN walks toward 77, his hand already extended. "It is a pleasure beyond anything I ever expected in my ho-hum life to meet you, Mr. Price. If you don't mind my saying, you are the luckiest man on the planet. Miss Mitchell is the finest woman, sir."

Malcolm smiles wide. "Gretchen, the kid stays. Do you need him, if not, I'd like to take him to the game room for a few?"

Researcher Randy bounces on his feet like an expectant 7-year old.

"Oh, for heaven's sake. Alright. Just hook up my computer and printer, then go have fun, Randy." After connecting this and that, the kid scampers down the hall. Gretchen rummages through the box, finds a file folder with an attached note from her father:

> **Gretchen,**
> **I spoke with Stacy Remington again this morning and updated her on the Dominique Brettenvue paternity issue. Manuel Xavier resides at the Rocco Fiancetti Compound, a clandestine and secure facility. Stacy suggests that anything you want sent to The Compound be sent to her and she will ensure that it is protected and delivered accordingly. The FBI agents at your location are aware of this protocol and will handle your mailings.**
> **Daddy**
> **P.S. I hope you are mending, and I approve of your suitor.**

The 'mending' daughter smiles wide at the note from the new and improved Granger Mitchell. She inches her way down the couch toward her computer and finger-pecks a legal memorandum with her unslung hand:

> **To: Manuel Xavier**
> **Subject: Dominique Brettenvue**
> **Dear Mr. Xavier,**
> **Our firm represents the above-named individual in a matter concerning paternity and custody of her unborn child. Please contact Attorney Gretchen Mitchell, or Attorney Granger Mitchell, at one of the numbers listed on the letterhead.**
> **Sincerely,**
> **Gretchen Mitchell**
> **Attorney – Mitchell and Morgan**

The Attorney sends the letter to print, puts it into a Mitchell and Morgan envelope, puts that into a certified mailing envelope, and walks it to the FBI agent standing at the elevator, "Agent, have you received a directive about outgoing mail?"

"Yes, ma'am."

She nods and smiles, "This is for delivery." With that taken care of Gretchen heads to the game room and stands at the doorway.

"...when you threw that three-pointer at the buzzer during Game 7 of the Finals, I knew it was going in—when you fell, I knew your career was over. I was more upset by that, Mr. Price, than I was happy about going OT with the Heat," the fan says with a shake of his head.

"Me, too, kid."

Randy points to Malcolm's 77 jersey behind glass and frame. "That's the shirt you wore that night—you framed it without cleaning it."

"Yeah."

"I would've done that too," Randy says with a note of camaraderie.

Malcolm feels Gretchen's presence. He turns and finds the woman he's in love with standing in the doorway. "You shouldn't be up."

Gretchen nods. "Actually, I think I'm going to take a nap. Randy, I left a list of things, mostly research things. If you brought your company laptop use it, but if not, use mine. There's probably enough work for several hours. I should be awake by then. Malcolm can you set him up somewhere to work, and maybe feed him?"

"Feed him? Damn, Miss Mitchell, that's some cold stuff, right there. Feed him, like I'm some…"

"Come on kid," Malcom says.

Researcher Randy walks from the room next to Gretchen, "Malcolm Price just called me kid."

Gretchen laughs.

Woman, take a breath.

The Rocco Fiancetti Compound sits on a thickly wooded, heavily guarded, 105-acre parcel in Shelburne County, Nova Scotia. The physical layout of The Compound consists of a multi-floor headquarters building, called the Main Cottage, a dozen cottage-style homes scattered throughout the wooded area, a NASA-worthy Computer Center, a just-completed state of the art Medical Center, an Athletic Center, various and sundry weapons training facilities, and bunkhouses for on-Compound trainees.

Former British Intelligence Operative, Rocco Fiancetti, converted the former MI6 safe house compound into home base for RFI. It is from The Compound that he and his assembled team of field detectives, cyber investigators and law enforcement specialists contract services out to governmental agencies and select clientele worldwide. Two RFI field detectives, Fred Serpico and Manuel Xavier, are recently back from a serial killer investigation. One returned with a GSW and a busted up back — the other returned to a stack of mail — most of which he has chosen to ignore.

LewPen

Dominique enters the lawyer's meeting room to find Granger Mitchell waiting for her—she was expecting Gretchen Mitchell. The prisoner casts a glance at the CO standing inside the room—it isn't the one who was at the meeting the week before. Dominique waits to be seated and chained before turning cold eyes toward Granger. "Where is Gretchen? Are you here because you found out that she and I..." Dominique stops herself from saying more.

"Gretchen had an accident last week after your meeting."

"Alvarez?" Dominique deflates.

Granger nods.

"Did she survive the assassination attempt?" Dominique asks with hopeful anticipation.

Granger nods.

Dominique bows her head. "I'm glad. Why are you here, Granger?"

"To tell you that Manuel Xavier has been sent correspondence concerning your unborn child."

"Does this visit mean you agree that my baby should be kept away from Celia and Benton Brettenvue?"

Granger nods. "Most assuredly."

"They will sue you when they find out you betrayed them," Dominique warns.

"I assure you. They will not."

"You have something on them?"

"If your parents pursue legal action against me, I have plenty on them; if they continue their pursuit of your baby, our law firm will file a counterclaim against them on your behalf. I'm quite sure you can think of a few things that would go against them in a court of law." Granger floats the balloon.

"You don't like my parents," Dominique confirms.

"Your father. I don't like what I've learned about his treatment of you."

Dominique shifts a bit. "Benton pimped me out the first time, Granger. I returned thereafter, I was a willing participant." She watches for a reaction. She receives none. "I appreciate that you want to think of me as a victim, but I would rather you put the screws to Benton and Celia. If you choose to do so, I am a willing participant." Dominique smiles.

So close…

Antonio Alvarez's goon waits outside the penitentiary walls for Granger Mitchell. "Time for the big shot lawyer to meet his maker," the goon snarls. "El diablo awaits you, Mr. Mitchell." While the eager killer waits for his next murder victim to leave his meeting with prisoner BOP-PA-555925, he places a call to Alvarez's ace in the hole.

Benton Brettenvue takes the incoming call, "What the fuck do you want?"

"Mr. Alvarez is calling in his debts, Mr. Brettenvue. He has a request — it is of the non-negotiable type. You and your wife will be dead upon your refusal, or in the event that you are unable to deliver, so to speak," the hitman laughs. "Mr. Alvarez has learned that you are pursuing custody of Dominique's baby. If you should prevail in your quest, you will surrender the baby to the family of Antonio Alvarez. If you do not deliver the child to Peru, within seven days of your gaining custody, Dominique dies in prison, and you and your bitch wife die elsewhere, all at the direction of Antonio Alvarez." The goon waits for push back. None comes. "I will tell Mr. Alvarez that you will grant his request." The goon hangs up. Had he listened a bit longer he would have heard the sound of a whiskey bottle sailing across a room and shattering into a thousand pieces.

...and, yet so far.
Granger Mitchell places a call to Benton Brettenvue from the comforts of his idling Buick in the parking lot of a federal penitentiary for women. The man who answers the lawyer's call is in an agitated state—it is about to get worse.

"Did the felon meet with anyone from your firm, yet?" Benton snarls.

"I met with Dominique this morning."

Benton drunk-laughs. "You're kidding! The almighty Granger Mitchell, Attorney at Law, spent time at LewPen?" he laughs a bit more. "Looking for a woman? Well, good for you, Granger. There's been talk, you know. It's been a very long time since Delaney." Benton waits for the rise he hopes to get. Granger's silence directs Benton back to the original topic of conversation. "Did you get the custody situation handled to our favor?" the drunkard slurs.

"Quite the opposite, Benton. Dominique is going to block your attempts for custody. She will be provided legal representation by my firm. Before you go issuing threats of legal action against me, know this, I have the goods on you for multiple federal and state crimes. If I have overplaycd my hand and cannot assemble enough evidence against you, Dominique has everything she could ever need to make sure you and Celia join her in the penitentiary for the remainder of your shameful lives. Good day, Benton." Granger Mitchell disconnects the call.

Brettenvue flips his shit.

The hitman watches two Discovery Land Rovers pull into the penitentiary parking lot. They drive along the row of cars, heading past the backend of Granger Mitchell's navy blue Buick Regal, one Rover takes the corner and passes by Granger's car and waits. The lawyer pulls from his parking space, moves behind the Discovery and waits for the second Discovery to close ranks behind him. The three vehicles leave in procession for the trip back to Philadelphia.

Killer goon flips his shit.

275

Gretchen is flying high after hearing about the meeting her father had with Dominique, then goes over the moon when she hears about the phone call with Benton. She heads in search of her man with good news to share. She finds him in his office sitting at a table by the window, on the phone. He waves her in. Gretchen stands across the room from Him, instantly surprised by how good he looks in this setting. It dawns on her that she hasn't spent any measurable amount of time in Malcolm's office—she uses the few minutes she has now to admire the place. Every piece of furniture is custom-made, "Most likely because of Malcolm's height." Upon further inspection, she notices certain style elements in the pieces. "The elevated section of his desk allows him to stand while working. Hmm, he always stands, usually against a wall. I wonder if there are lingering issues from his knee injury?" Gretchen walks the perimeter of the room looking at this plaque and that award, all of them in recognition of his service to one civic organization or another.

When she comes upon the key to the borough of Lewisburg, she remembers a conversation they had the first night they slept together…

"Why do you work at the prison?" she asked.

"Penitentiary," he corrected.

"Seriously, Malcolm, I'd like to know why."

"Are you asking me why I work at all or why I work there in particular?"

"There."

"I'm at the women's wing of the penitentiary because there are too many men behind bars that would love to make a name by killing a former NBA star."

Gretchen nodded. "Now for the other question, why are you working a nine to five job at all?"

"I have plans for later in life, so while I wait for later, I'm earning an honest day's pay for an honest day's work."

"Do you feel like sharing what your 'later in life' plans are?"

"Politics," was all he said.

Malcolm interrupts Gretchen's thoughts. "Woman, you're deep in..."

She struts his way, crawls onto his lap, and presses her bottom onto his erection. "You're awfully excited, Mr. Price. Were you on the phone with, 'Oh, Baby 555-1324?'"

Malcolm pushes himself against her bottom. "I saw you. I want you."

Gretchen gets off Malcolm's lap and takes hold of his hand. "I saw you. I want you."

"You healed enough? I don't want to hurt you."

"Then gentle me, Malcolm," Gretchen tugs him to his feet.

The MAN gentles the WOMAN in the shower bringing her to within a breath of orgasm. He dries her off, takes her into his arms and to his bed. He lays beside her, touching, stroking, petting until she is once again near release. He lifts her onto his desperately aching erection. "Go slow, Gretchen. It's been awhile," he groans.

"I'm so close Malcolm." She eases onto him – onto all of him. The nearing-man takes hold of Gretchen's hips to try to slow her. She will have none of it. "Malcolm, I need you. All of you. Please," Gretchen moans. He lets go of her hips and lets his woman take what she needs then gives her every ounce of what he has. Gretchen collapses on top, her face nestled against his neck. She breathes him in—lets him fill every place of her heart. When she can, she sits up and traces her fingers across his face, drops her hand and cradles her throbbing elbow with an, "Ouch."

"Woman?"

"It's nothing. Really, Malcolm. You don't need to worry…" It dawns on her that he hasn't left her side since the assassination attempt.

"Malcolm, you haven't been back to work since the accident."

"I quit."

"You what?"

"I was planning on giving my notice June 1st. I decided this isn't the time for me to be away from you, Gretchen."

She crawls off him and sits crossed-legged facing him, "What are you going to do with your time?"

He smiles devilishly, "I can think of a variety of things to keep me busy." He tries to pull her to him; she slaps him away.

"Are you going into politics, Malcolm Price? I mean you told me once that was part of your life's plan, and then we never discussed it, probably because someone tried to kill me, or perhaps because we seem to spend our time doing other things, but maybe we should discuss your plans because if you are going into politics it's a messy business and …"

"Woman, take a breath." He laughs, a good, hearty laugh. "Yes, politics is most definitely in my plans, if the citizens of the great city of Lewisburg want me."

Gretchen hops onto her knees, "You want to be mayor of Lewisburg?"

"I want to be Governor of Pennsylvania, but I'll start by being mayor of Lewisburg."

"Oh, Malcolm," Gretchen squeals. "You'd be a wonderful mayor and governor, and you are a shoo-in with the ladies, unless they don't like that you are with a woman, a white woman to boot. Do you think that will matter, because if you think so, we should maybe change our personal plans, oh, but I don't want to change them because I love you Malcolm, but maybe I should love you enough to let you have your dream, oh, Malcolm I just don't ..."

Malcolm lays Gretchen onto her back. "I think I need to find a way to shut you up, Woman. Any suggestions?"

"You could kiss me."

Malcolm kisses her then gentles her until she's speechless.

What's with the upper crust?

Weeks have passed since Gretchen sent her first legal Memorandum to Manuel Xavier. Since then, she has forwarded three identical pieces of correspondence each week, to which she has received no response.

During that same period of time, Granger Mitchell has visited with Dominique every Wednesday. They spend their time working on a counterclaim, should they receive legal action from the Brettenvues. When notification comes that the Brettenvue's have made their move, the attorney and the prisoner are left gobsmacked:

Benton and Celia Brettenvue request
visitation with
Lewisburg Penitentiary inmate,
BOP-PA-555925 aka Dominique Brettenvue.

Their request is denied.

The Compound
Manuel Xavier opens a business envelope that bears a 3x3 inch return address from a law firm in Philadelphia, Pennsylvania. He reads the first two lines…

To: Manuel Xavier
Subject: Dominique Brettenvue

He folds the paper, puts it back into the envelope, puts it and the handful of others like it into a kitchen drawer, and slams it shut.

Muriel Dermot, the very new girlfriend – houseguest – of Manuel Xavier, nearly jumps off the sofa at the sudden noise behind her. From across the room, she feels raw seething emotion roiling off him. "Wow, whatever's in those letters set you off."

"Didn't read the letters," he scoffs.

She chuckles, "And you're this angry without even reading them?"

"They are about Dominique."

"Oh. There sure are a lot of them, Manuel."

"Your point?"

"Whoever is sending them is going to keep sending them. Do you think you should…"

Manuel bends over his companion and kisses the top of her head pulling in her soft floral musky scent. "No, I do not think I should read them."

Washington, DC
FICA Director Stacy Remington receives the third call from Granger Mitchell in as many weeks to ask for a favor. She grants his request. Stacy Remington places a phone call to Rocco Fiancetti.

"Ah, Director Remington, it is with pleasurable feelings to hear from you," Rocco says in his kitschy Italian.

"I wish this were a pleasure call, but I'm afraid I have news. I need to say it is not professional in nature, Rocco, may I proceed?"

"Si, but of course, Stacy."

"I received a call this morning from Attorney Granger Mitchell out of Philadelphia. An attorney with his firm, Gretchen Mitchell, is representing Dominique Brettenvue in a paternity and custody case regarding her unborn child. Ms. Brettenvue has instructed Attorney Mitchell to contact the father of said child; Ms. Mitchell has sent several letters to Manuel."

There is a long pause on Rocco's end. "Grazi, Stacy."

Manuel and Muriel are relaxing together on the couch in his cottage—he is kissing her neck, she is making notes for a new book—when there comes a knock on the door. Manuel calls, "Come on in," never expecting that the visitor would be his father. Manuel scrambles to his feet nearly tossing Muriel onto the floor upon sight of Rocco Fiancetti. "Are you lost, Papa? You've never been here before. I did not know you knew where I live."

Rocco addresses Muriel, "Excuse us, please."

Muriel smiles and heads toward the back bedroom. Rocco touches her arm. "Please go to the Main Cottage."

Muriel smiles and throws a 'good luck' look toward Manuel. He questions his father, "What's with the upper crust?"

When the door shuts behind Muriel, Rocco says four words, "Where are the letters?"

"What letters?"

"Mitchell and Morgan letters, from Philadelphia," Rocco clarifies.

Manuel walks to the kitchen and retrieves the letters in discussion.

"Have you read them?" Rocco asks, an uncharacteristic seethe emanating from the man.

Manuel shakes his head. "No."

"Dominique says you are papa to her child."

Manuel tears open the letters.

275 Market Street

Gretchen has been out of sorts for the past few days. Her captivity has left her stir-crazy, fresh-air deprived, and *really* pissed off that she hasn't heard from Manuel Xavier. When her phone rings, displaying an unknown number, she almost doesn't answer. She catches the call just before it goes to voicemail.

"Gretchen Mitchell."

"Miss Mitchell, this is Manuel Xavier. I believe you are trying to reach me."

Gretchen scrambles to her feet and begins pacing. "Yes, Mr. Xavier, thank you for calling. I am representing..."

"Excuse my interruption, Miss Mitchell, but I am aware of the reasons for your letters. Your father contacted FICA Director, Stacy Remington, who contacted my father, Rocco Fiancetti. Several people have gone to a lot of trouble to reach me. I believe your client may be manipulating you for some reason. Dominique assured me, rather gleefully, and while holding a loaded gun to my head, that Antonio Alvarez is her child's father."

"My client said she lied to you about the paternity, and that there is proof, a paternity test that names you as the father, Mr. Xavier."

"Call me Manuel."

"And I'm, Gretchen. Like I said, Dominique said she has proof."

"What proof?"

"There is a paternity test result inside a plastic bag, hidden in the northeast corner of a guard shack near Pascal and Coco's cottage. She said you will know what that means and that you should check beneath the loose floorboard."

"I'll call you back." Manuel hangs up.

Two hours pass with no word.

Malcolm returns from Mama Girl's treatment to find a whirling dervish where his woman used to be. He soon learns that Gretchen is waiting for a call about a "damned plastic bagged paternity test stuffed into the northeast corner of a guard shack in the middle of a super-spy compound in the middle of nowhere land." The laughing man tries to pull his woman for a hug—he finds her as huggable as a porcupine.

"Malcolm, I don't need a hug, I need a damned phone call," she swats him away.

"Woman, you need more than that. You're making me dizzy. Sit yourself."

As soon as she sits the phone rings, and she is back on her feet pacing the room. "Gretchen Mitchell."

"I found it. How do we prove its valid?" Manuel asks.

"We run another paternity test, here in Pennsylvania. The situation is time sensitive, the baby is due at the beginning of June. I can have the necessary paperwork for the paternity test done by the end of the week. Could you be here Friday? Before you answer, you should know that Dominique's parents have expressed interest in gaining custody of the baby, and Antonio Alvarez is a threat, as well, since he is on record as being the father."

"I'll be there Friday. Will I be seeing Dominique?"

"Not to establish paternity, but during the signing of custody papers, assuming paternity is established."

"Where will you and I meet, Gretchen?"

"The thing is, I am currently in protective custody after an assassination attempt by Antonio Alvarez. Federal agents will need to get you from the airport and escort you to my location. The cheek swab will be done here under the supervision of legal authorities, and then you can be on your way. As you are former FBI I'm sure you understand."

"Better than you think. If Alvarez put a hit on you, you are in some deep shit, Gretchen. Call me when you get everything worked out with the paternity test." Manuel disconnects the call.

Gretchen goes to Malcolm to get her hug. It isn't the greatest hug, in fact, it's hardly a hug at all. "Is something wrong, Malcolm?"

He is deep in a memory...

"There's an FBI agent downstairs. He said he's here about Sage."

"Shit."

FICA Agent, Manuel Xavier, was waiting in the foyer for Malcolm Price. After an introduction he pointed to luggage that was set at the front door, "Are you coming or going, Mr. Price?"

Malcolm laughed, "I haven't been here in years. I show up. You show up. I'm sure you know the answer to your question. But since you asked, I'm going home."

"To Lewisburg."

"Why are you here, Agent Xavier?"

"An internet hacker-for-hire named Stoner Strong did a deep dive on you during the 2007 playoffs. Did you know anything about that, Mr. Price?"

"Not until Detective Romney mentioned it during his questioning of me in 2007."

"Any idea why the nephew of Micky Strong had a fascination with you?"

"You know the answer to that question, Agent Xavier. I think we're done, here. Correction: I'm done."

"Malcolm," Gretchen says again and with a nudge.

He shakes off his thoughts and gives the whole hugging thing another go of it, "Come here, Woman." He wraps his arms and kisses her temple as the name Manuel Xavier bangs through his head.

Gretchen snuggles into his embrace, "Now. That's better."

Until he gets his mark.

Gretchen greets Manuel at the privacy elevator. She extends her hand in introduction, "Gretchen Mitchell, it's nice to meet you, Manuel. I hope your trip was pleasurable," she says through her million-watt smile.

He nods, "Your security set-up looks good, Gretchen, but you need some more on the outer perimeter by the back entrance, unless you are luring your assassin to that location as part of a capture plan. Not a criticism, just occupational bossiness," Manuel says.

"I'd like you to tell Captain Johnson your opinion, if you don't mind," Malcolm says as he crosses the living room with outstretched hand.

"Malcolm Price."

"Manuel Xavier."

The men recognize one another,
neither says so.

Gretchen pushes in. "Why don't you take a seat, Manuel. Captain Damian Johnson, who is point on this security detail will be accompanying Physician's Assistant, Wanda Johnson, and an FBI notary public to this meeting." The woman hip-chucks the former b-baller making sure he caught her seamless use of a basketball reference.

"You can take point later, Woman," he growls low.

She brightens then continues to address Manuel, "They will be here in a few minutes to oversee the paternity test and the signing of legal documents. You should be on your way within the hour."

Manuel takes the offered seat, and Gretchen joins him. Malcolm takes his customary lean against a wall. Manuel veers off topic. "Before making the trip, Gretchen, I asked Director Remington, my former boss at FICA, to forward me the file on the assassination attempt made against you. I read it on the plane. Alvarez put a 'don't stop' contract on you, I assume you are aware of this?"

"Yes. Captain Johnson has informed us about the seriousness of the situation."

Manuel scoffs, "No disrespect to the captain, but I doubt any of you really know about the seriousness of this situation."

"You know things about Antonio Alvarez?" Malcolm asks.

"Too many things. My last undercover assignment with the FBI put me deep into Alvarez's operation. I assume you're aware that Alvarez and his associates attempted to kidnap the top three ranked cyber huntresses to keep as work-slaves for The Realm."

Gretchen nods. "You'd have to be living under a rather big rock not to have heard about The Realm."

Manuel laughs. "Alvarez's people managed to kidnap cyber huntress, FICA Agent, Hannah Leavy. She was minutes away from being loaded onto an LNG tanker heading to Peru where Alvarez and several other Realm leaders were waiting her arrival. My team managed to get her away from her kidnappers."

Malcolm imposes. "If you have time after your business with Gretchen, you might speak with Captain Johnson. Maybe you could help with something other than an assessment on perimeter security. We would appreciate the assist."

The ping of the arriving elevator puts one discussion on hold, and another into play. After introductions, a few signatures on documents, and a cheek swab, the law enforcers head to the game room. Malcom gets the conversation started. "I explained some of what you said about Antonio Alvarez to Captain Johnson. Let's figure out a way to get Gretchen out of this mess."

"Captain Johnson, I have a pretty good sense of what happened in the garage. I noticed security cameras on my way up. Did you get anything useful?"

"Plenty of visuals from street cameras of the black Escalade passing by the apartment building, but the windows on the Escalade are tinted, so there are no facials. The images of the BMW used in the attack are grainy. Forensics is working on facial recognition, but nothing so far."

"Any chance I can see the footage?"

"At the station, but I have stills with me." Captain Johnson removes several pictures from his pocket. "We need an ID on this guy." He hands Manuel the pictures. The former undercover FBI Agent flips through. He remains silent on his first reviews, confirms on his third.

"Cappa Escobar. The pictures are grainy, but I recognize the bastard."

Captain Johnson reaches into his pocket for his cell, Manuel stops him. "Hold up a minute, Captain. When I spoke with Director Remington earlier, I suggested Alvarez would have hired Escobar for this hit. Her intel has Cappa Escobar in Guatemala—so there's a problem with that, but now that we know he's here, we can prepare for his next move. Escobar failed on his first attempt, that's gonna Piss. Him. Off. More to the point, it's going to push him to come back around, and he won't be as subtle next time. The attempt in the garage is classic Escobar. His typical crime scenes don't look like typical crime scenes. Case in point, his plan for Gretchen was for her to have an 'accident' in the garage. Things will be different the next time around— he's gonna come loaded for bear. You should expect him sooner rather than later, and plan on him swinging around until the job is done. Cappa contracts himself out for $2 Million a whack, and clears his schedule for six months. He usually gets things done within a month, but he'll stay with it until he gets his mark."

"So, what's the plan?"

"The first part is to keep the Feds away. I suggest you keep the agents you have, but limit it to them. If you call Remington and tell her it's Escobar, she's going to do one of two things. Flood this place with agents, which will send Escobar underground, or take Gretchen out of here, and squirrel her away someplace…"

"Director Remington…"

"Made a deal with Granger Mitchell that Gretchen could stay here. She told me. The thing is, Director Remington's hands will be tied when the brass learns Escobar is the one trying to kill a prosecution witness against Antonio Alvarez. They cannot let that happen, and they cannot let the press learn that Antonio Alvarez contracted an assassination from behind the concrete and steel of the ADX Supermax in Colorado, The shit will it the fan if that happens. FBI Director Webber won't care about Remington's deal with Granger Mitchell—she will take Gretchen. She's probably gonna take her anyway. This place is huge, and it presents logistical problems, not to mention the cost of all of this. It is way more cost effective to put her someplace with two agents protecting her.

Given all that, I say we get this ball rolling with Escobar. Let's lure him to the least secure place here," Manuel smiles.

Captain Johnson smiles. "The back of the apartment building."

The men nod.

"Tell me, Manuel, do you need to get back to RFI right away?"

"Nope. I'm yours if you need me, Captain. I'd love to be around when Cappa Escobar goes down."

The unexpected, but very much appreciated, and appropriately armed houseguest grabs his overnight gear from the Fed's SUV in the garage and follows Malcolm to the guest suite off the game room. "Director Remington's interest in this case – care to explain?"

"Gretchen's father has a personal relationship with Stacy Remington. It's a significant relationship," Malcolm offers.

Manuel nods, "She made it clear that I should press in with Captain Johnson. Director Remington does not show her cards—EVER. It was obvious that this case is causing her concern."

Malcolm nods.

Manuel nods.

The men wait through a bit of silence. It's not a long wait.

"Speaking of…are you going to tell Gretchen that we know each other?"

"We weren't speaking of that, Manuel."

"Nope, but we should be."

Malcolm shakes his head. "Not the time for that story, Manuel."

The visitor shakes his head. "Your call, man."

Within minutes, the men join Gretchen in the kitchen. She prepares lunch while the men talk basketball. The conversation quickly turns to Gretchen's favorite topic—that she didn't know who Malcolm Price was when they first started dating.

"Must have been a really big rock you were living under, Gretchen, not to have heard about 77." Manuel tossed back her previous words about The Realm. She laughs. He continues. "This man has so much print on him, the Library of Congress probably has a designated Malcolm Price wing," he teases.

"Yeah, yeah, Malcolm Price was big shit," Gretchen teases back.

"**Is** big shit, Woman," Malcolm corrects.

Gretchen gives her man a huge smile and a raised brow. The 'not so subtle' reference is not lost on Manuel, who cracks up. "Well, okay, that was easy to catch," he says as he excuses himself to make a call.

Gretchen w.a.t.c.h.e.s. Manuel's backside as he walks away, stretching far to w.a.t.c.h. every-last-step-he-takes.

"What are you looking at, Woman?"

"Your replacement if you don't behave," she teases.

"You'll never replace me, Gretchen."

"Never could, Malcolm."

The lovers are loving a bit when Manuel returns. "Sorry to interrupt. I can take my lunch elsewhere if you two have business to attend."

"Nope. Nope. No business here," Gretchen smirks.

"Need to keep my Woman unwound, is all. She's starting to go stir-crazy."

"Then let's get Escobar," Manuel suggests.

Carry on, Alice.

At sunrise, Manuel takes a seat on a bench at Hufnagle Park. The former undercover agent pretends to read the Union County newspaper while he enjoys a morning cup of Joe. What he's really doing is watching Cappa Escobar pace Market Street before circling around to the back of the brick face building at 275. Manuel puts down his paper and coffee and places a call to RFI's lead field detective, Fred Serpico, who's just finished an IOD stint and is eager to be back out in the field.

"It's early, Manuel."

"I'm sitting across the street from the building owned by Malcolm Price."

"Didn't know you were a fan of 77— apparently a weird fan of 77?"

"Not the point, Fred."

"What's the point, Manuel?"

"There's a woman who lives with Price— there's a 'don't stop' contract on her."

"Who's the woman?"

"A lawyer named Gretchen Mitchell."

"A lawyer, huh? Probably explains the 'don't stop' order," he laughs

Manuel laughs, "Yeah, it explains it, but in a weird way…"

Fred interrupts, "The word weird has come up twice already, and I've been awake for two minutes?"

"Fred. Listen. Antonio Alvarez put the hit on Ms. Mitchell because she is providing legal representation to Dominique."

"I thought Dominique was tucked away and doing life at LewPen. What's the basis of the legal representation?"

"Paternity and custody of Dominique's baby."

A fraction-of–a-fraction-of–a-second passes before Fred laughs. BIG!
"Congratulations, Daddy."

"Not the point, Fred."

"What's the point, Manuel?"

"I've got a hitman—one of the best hitmen in the business—preparing his entrance point at Price's building for his second assassination attempt against Gretchen Mitchell."

"I'm on my way."

Manuel gets back to his paper and coffee. He waits for Escobar to leave the back alley and the general vicinity, then sneaks into 275. "Escobar is here," Manuel tells Malcolm with no preamble. "He was just at the back of the building, probably working the locks, if he's true to form he'll return after midnight. I placed a call to RFI and asked an associate to join me, he'll be here in a few hours. The Feds downstairs will get him from the airport and send him up. You should call Captain Johnson and ask him to come over, and to keep a low profile. We don't want Escobar to wonder if something's up. Where's Gretchen?"

"Still sleeping. She had some trouble getting that way last night."

"Let her sleep, she's gonna be up all night," Manuel says before heading to the shower. When Manuel joins Malcolm back in the game room he smirks at the off-pitch destruction being done to Lesley Gore's classic *You Don't Own Me.* "Your woman sings—and I use that term loosely—as though she doesn't know you own her, man."

"She knows."

Manuel laughs, "By the way, does she know what's up with Escobar?"

"Nope. Let's tell her when Damian gets here."

Fred Serpico and Damian Johnson arrive at the penthouse mid-afternoon. They ride the elevator together and emerge into the penthouse as besties. After Manuel introduces Fred to Malcolm and Gretchen, the men get busy devising the trap for Cappa Escobar. They work the logistics of who goes where and does what, disengage part of the security system, then travel the staircase making sure Escobar has easy access to the top floor. Malcolm hands Damian a set of keys, "The master unlocks the main access door at ground level and at each floor. The other keys gain access to the penthouse from the staircase and the elevator in case the security keypad isn't working." He leaves the men in the game room and goes in search of Gretchen. He finds her in the kitchen, stirring this, chopping that, and rattling a fair share of pots and pans.

"Woman."

She stops her rattling with an, "Ouch."

"Forgot your injured elbow?"

"Forgot to include the 'Little Lady' in on the plan? You know, the person who is the intended victim of the assassin. I'll remind you, Mr. Price, that Cappa Escobar was no match for me the first go round. Please share that fact with the other misogynists in the game room."

Malcolm pushes off the brick wall he favors and moves toward Gretchen. He stops when she raises a pan in threat.

"Ouch."

"Forgot your injured elbow," he smiles.

Gretchen moves the pan to her other hand and raises it, "You might consider taking the wall again since I'm ambidextrous."

"I'll take my chances," he says as he closes the space between them.

She lowers the pan and folds into his arms.

"No one's doubting your capabilities, Gretchen. There's a game plan, and you'll be part of it."

"But you'll be taking point," she scoffs.

"Nope. Manuel is point on this. His team, of which you are a member, will do what he says, when he says. Got it?"

She relaxes in his arms, "Got it."

He taps her ass with his gigantic paw, "Good, now fix some dinner, Little Lady."

She spins, raises her ambidextrous pan holding hand high, "Best be leaving now Malcolm."

"Yes, ma'am."

Gretchen serves a "man's meal" of T-bone steaks and baked spuds. Whilst she serves, the men lay out the plan. She listens. She ponders. She asks... "What makes you think Escobar is coming back?"

"The 'don't stop' order," the men say in unison.

"What makes you think he's coming back *tonight*?"

The men answer this question around mouthfuls of food.

"Escobar probably thinks the local cops labeled the events in the garage an accident..."

"...because Escobar makes his hits look like accidents..."

"…and when the police activity died down after the first night…"

"…and the Feds didn't storm 275…"

"…and Captain Johnson kept them on a tight rein…"

"…Escobar started thinking he was in the clear and started planning his second attempt…"

"…that gives us two advantages against Escobar…"

"…he doesn't know Attorney Howard gave a heads up about the contract hit…"

"…and he doesn't know you are under protective custody…"

"…he probably thinks you're on the downlow because you're recuperating…"

"…which is why he's going to take his second whack at you…"

"…sooner rather than later."

Gretchen listens. Gretchen ponders. Gretchen asks… "If we know Escobar is coming for me, why lure him inside 275? Why don't you just ambush him in the alleyway, or on the stairs?"

"It needs to be clear that Escobar is making a move on you…"

"…arresting him outside or even on the stairs inside isn't good enough…"

"…he has to be inside the penthouse."

Gretchen listens. Gretchen ponders. Gretchen asks… "I don't suppose my death will be the result of an accident this time, perhaps a slip and fall in the shower."

"Nope. He plans on shooting you," the men say in unison.

Gretchen is sitting on the living room couch minding her own business when the men descend upon her from the game room. She stops scrolling through her memos and listens to the conversation going on around her—a conversation intended to get a rise out of her.

"You work at LewPen, right?" Manuel asks.

"Until last week," Malcolm nods.

"You armed, here?"

"If need be."

"Need be. Get your gear."

Gretchen is rendered speechless when Malcolm walks past her, unlocks the center section of the sideboard, takes out a gun safe, works a combination, removes two handguns, checks them, loads them, tucks one into the waistband of his jeans and straps one into a holster that is already affixed to his ankle.

"You p-p-pack heat?"

Malcolm smiles wide. "All kinds of heat, Woman." He walks to her and k.i.s.s.e.s. her, then heads to the kitchen to join Manuel, Fred, and Damian—who are thoroughly enjoying the show. After a minute of good fun, the men stop talking and lock eyes on Gretchen who is kneeling on the couch and peering over its back.

"What are you doing, Woman?"

"Looking for a white rabbit, a Cheshire cat, and a playing card queen, of course."

"Carry on Alice," Malcolm laughs at his woman.

Escobar coming in.

Lights go out at 11 PM at 275 Market Street.

Malcolm, Gretchen and Fred are in the living room—the elevator door is open and locked in place—an ominous reminder that the shit is about to hit the fan. Don Patterson, an FBI agent with whom Manuel has worked in the past is positioned in the alley behind Malcom's building, as primary lookout. Captain Johnson and one of his men are behind a hallway access door on the sixth floor. Lewisburg police are stationed inside the hallways on floors 2-7 to handle tenant movement. FBI agents lay in wait inside the parking garage preventing anyone from entering the building. Manuel is positioned just inside the penthouse at the eighth floor landing.

At 2:30 AM the team receives a text from the alleyway agent.
Escobar coming in.

Cappa Escobar closes the door behind him. He inches to the stairs, leans against a railing and looks upward. He climbs to the first landing, leans against the railing and looks upward. He pauses, he listens, he reviews his plan, "Get in, get Price, get the puta, get the fuck out."

Malcolm and Fred pocket their cell phones after reading the text. "Escobar is here," Malcolm says as he pulls Gretchen to her feet. He kisses the top of her head, "Go."

Fred and Gretchen enter the elevator. When the door closes behind them, the RFI operative locks the elevator down. He reminds Gretchen, "Escobar isn't expecting the fire power we've got assembled, and since he likes to work alone, he's probably going to be alone. If that's the case, he won't make it as far as the living room." Fred steps in front of Gretchen to pull her full attention. "I want you to listen to me, Gretchen. If the living room is breached, this elevator goes to the garage and you and I get out of 275. Do you understand?"

"But Malcolm is positioned in the living room."

"No buts, Gretchen."

The rest of the team gets in place.

Agent Patterson moves to his position outside the alley door.

Captain Johnson and his man wait behind the sixth floor access hallway door.

Manuel tucks into a corner just inside the entranceway to the penthouse.

Malcolm presses against a far wall opposite the elevator.

Escobar continues his climb. and his routine. At each landing, a lean against the railing, a look upward, a pause, a listen, a review of his plan. "Get in, get Price, get the puta, get the fuck out." At the fifth floor landing he freezes. He closes his eyes, listens, assesses. "Muffled sounds…a theme song…a television show." He pulls a breath and moves to the next floor—the sixth floor. He stops at the landing, leans against the railing, takes a look upward, *and* a look downward. He starts up the stairs, then abruptly stops. A push of concern hits deep—a chill runs his spine—he pushes back against the nudge of doubt. "Alvarez wants this done. Kill the lawyer, send a message to the Brettenvues—all of them! No one defies Alvarez—not even me." He reviews his plan again, "Get in, get Price, get the puta, get the fuck out."

Manuel feels the hitman's arrival.

The hitman makes his move.

Escobar settles on the eighth floor landing. He gets what he needs to bump the lock, stands upright when he hears the click, pockets the bump key, and waits a second before turning the knob. The contract killer enters the penthouse. He realizes he is in a trap a-fraction-of–a-fraction-of–a-second before Manuel Xavier springs it.

"Drop your weapon, Cappa, you're surrounded."

"Manuel Xavier," Cappa snarls at the sound of the former FBI agent's voice. "Mr. Alvarez will be pleased to know that you die tonight along with the puta." Escobar swings his arm toward Manuel, both men fire.

Gretchen freaks when she hears the shots. Fred calms her, "It's not Malcolm. The shots came from farther away, maybe the stairwell. I need you to keep it together, Gretchen, I need to listen," he takes hold of her hand.

Escobar scrambles from the room toward the stairs, blood dripping behind him. From the stair leading to the eight floor, Captain Johnson orders Escobar to stop. Escobar swings his arm toward Damian Johnson, both men fire. Two men fall. Manuel races to Escobar, kicks his weapon away. Captain Johnson's man goes to his aid, talking into his shoulder walkie that an officer is down at 275 Market Street, rear entrance.

Gretchen slides to the floor at the second round of gunfire. She wraps her arms around her legs and buries her head into them. That is how

FBI Agent Patterson finds her when he uses the access key to open the elevator door. Fred extends his hand to Gretchen, listens to the professional.

"Escobar is dead on the back stairs. Captain Johnson is headed to Geisinger Medical Center with life-threatening injuries. He's being followed by Xavier and Price. I've been dispatched to you as backup protection for Ms. Mitchell."

Fred feels Gretchen's hand begin to tremble and slacken. He leans into her and walks her to the couch. He can tell she's about to experience and adrenaline-crash. "It's been a long day, Gretchen. Why don't you sit yourself on the couch. I'll let you know as soon as I hear anything."

"Promise."

"Promise."

Manuel follows the ambulance down Market Street, then veers off and follows Malcolm's directions to a renovated brownstone just outside the city limits. The lifelong best friend of the critically injured captain bolts from the vehicle and pounds on Damian's door.

Wanda nearly rips the door from its hinges, "Who the hell..." She holds the rest of her tirade when she sees Malcolm's face. She pulls the door closed, races past him, and throws herself into the back of Manuel's ride. "Tell me," she directs.

"Captain Johnson got stuck on a set of stairs between a gunman and one of his officers. As best we can tell, Damian threw himself over a railing. He took a bullet to his thigh."

"The femoral?" Wanda asks.

Manuel pauses.

"Give it to me straight, Mr. Xavier."

"Given the blood loss, I'd say it's involved."

"Was he conscious?"

"No," Malcolm whispers.

Damian Johnson is in surgery when they arrive, and for the next several hours. At one point during their vigil, Wanda approaches Manuel who's lost in thought at the window. When he turns, she notices the blood — her husband's blood — on the man's clothing.

"You administered care."

He nods.

Malcolm speaks from behind them, "EMT's said Damian would have bled out without Manuel's help."

Wanda wraps her arms around Manuel. "Words fail me."

"That's a first," Malcolm teases.

"Don't need your input, Malcolm." She steps from Manuel's arms and places a hand to his cheek, "You will receive official notification tomorrow, but my words will suffice. The paternity test is conclusive, the baby girl Dominique Brettenvue is carrying is yours. Congratulations."

"The baby is a girl?" Manuel asks.

Wanda nods.

Manuel pulls the woman in for another hug. She breaks in his arms.

You named the baby, Charlotte.

Attorney Gretchen Mitchell waits with Manuel Xavier for inmate BOP-PA-555925 to enter the lawyer meeting room. Both are pacing the small area. They move to the wall farthest from the door when they hear a knock. They silently watch as Dominique is brought in, seated, and chained at the table. It isn't until the escorting CO steps away that the pretty woman with strawberry-blonde ringlets, and freckles across her nose lifts her eyes toward Manuel. "Will you keep our baby, or give her away?"

"I will raise her." Manuel moves to the table, sits across from the woman with whom he created a life. They stare at one another for many seconds before either speaks.

"I'm at peace with that, Manuel. Please don't tell our daughter I am the one who brought her into this world. At least, try to keep that from her, and please do not, under any circumstances, let Benton and Celia Brettenvue anywhere near this child," she manages to move her shackled hand to her baby bump, and give it a little swirl of her thumb.

"I promise to take care of her. Is there anything else, Dominique?" Manuel waits until she shakes her head, no. He leans toward her and speaks softly, "Ms. Mitchell said you named the baby, Charlotte?"

Dominique nods through a sudden rush of tears.

"Then, that will be our daughter's name." he says as his own eyes wet.

The overcome woman hangs her head as low as she can. After a few minutes, Gretchen replaces Manuel at the table, and explains the paperwork that each parent will sign. When she is finished, she asks *the* question. "Dominique Brettenvue, is it your intention to release your unborn daughter, Charlotte, to her father, Manuel Xavier, upon her birth?"

"Yes."

Two COs step forward. They unlock the prisoner's chains so that she is able to sign the papers. When Dominique Brettenvue is finished she hands the pen to Manuel. He takes hold of her hand and gently squeezes it.

"No touching," the CO barks.

Manuel Xavier signs the paperwork.

As Dominique is being led from the meeting room she addresses Manuel, "Thank you," she says with a smile reminiscent of the sweet woman he met on a plane to Belize.

June first.

    U.S. Bureau of Prisons inmate BOP-PA-555925, is handcuffed to a gurney located inside a locked prison clinic inside a women's federal penitentiary. She is pushing through the final stages of labor. Though quiet, she is in unbearable pain. She knows the physical pain will subside soon enough — just as she knows the emotional pain will never leave her. If anything, it will intensify as she lingers in her solitary confinement cell, the one that she'd turned into a beautiful French villa for her little girl.

    In a matter of minutes, Dominique Brettenvue will become a mother. According to the rules set by the Commonwealth of Pennsylvania, she will never lay eyes on her daughter, never hold her, never place a kiss upon her forehead. Her plight is of her own doing, but she had help in getting to where she is today. Exhausted from hours of labor, and unable to control her state, her daughter's name escapes on Dominique's panting breaths, "Charlotte." A thought circles through her head. It is one that she has **never** had before—*a woman, somewhere, labored through my birth.*

Who was she? Why did she give me away—to them?

After a few minutes and a few pushes, the baby known as Charlotte makes her entrance into the world. The newborn's first wail is answered by her mother's plaintive whisper,

"Goodbye, mon cheri."

The End

More to come …

Please enjoy the teaser for my next book in the series, *Resolutions…*

RESOLUTIONS

THE PUNISHER

--- PULLING THREADS ---

Book Nine

SHERYLL O'BRIEN

Thirty-five thousand feet in the air.

"Penny for your thoughts." Gretchen Mitchell whispers, then shoulder-nudges her travel companion, Malcolm Price. "You've been awfully quiet. Are you alright? Is it Damian? Do you want to go back to Lewisburg?"

The MAN with a broadening smile takes his woman's hand and kisses her knuckles, "Yes, I'm alright. Yes, I'm concerned about Damian. Yes, I want to go back to Lewisburg, but it's important that we take this time away." He follows the path of his woman's cornflower blue eyes. They land on two people who've just begun their journey in life — Manuel Xavier and the sweet little wonder born that afternoon at 3:33 PM, his daughter, Charlotte. "That's a sight," Malcolm smiles wide.

Gretchen silences a laugh when she sees the look on Manuel's face. "You okay, over there?"

"Do I look okay?"

"Nope. Nope. You look terrified, which is somewhat surprising considering you are…"

"A former Federal agent who infiltrated a criminal organization in Peru, kidnapped a kidnapped victim, pissed off a worldwide syndicate, hid out for months, and outlived a bounty."

"Yes – all that. How is it possible that you did all that, yet an itty-bitty baby has rendered you an unglued mess?"

"Haven't a clue." He looks at Charlotte, then looks back at Gretchen, "She's been asleep for hours. Are they supposed to sleep for hours?"

Gretchen laughs, "I don't know. The discharge nurse at the penitentiary said," Gretchen stalls, "well, **that** sure sounded strange. Anyway, the discharge nurse did a top to bottom exam, and the escort nurse fed and changed her before we boarded the jet, so I suspect all is well with Charlotte."

"I need her to sleep until we land."

"Then what?"

"I don't know. I'm hoping someone at The Compound will tell me what to do. Jesus, Gretchen. This kid needs a mother and a father. I am neither of those things."

"Well, that isn't entirely true, Manuel. You are one of those two things." She looks to Malcolm for some help. Nudges him when none is offered.

"What?"

"Say something."

"What?"

"I don't know. Say something reassuring."

"It's been five hours and she's still alive."

Manuel places his palm onto Charlotte's tiny head and whispers,

"Good God, it's only been five hours?"

ABOUT THE AUTHOR

She is not dead.

Sheryll O'Brien crafts characters without constraints. She tells them who they are, then let's them show her better versions of themselves. She gives them life and they live it beyond her wildest dreams.

Sheryll is a lifelong resident of Worcester, Massachusetts, where she is wife to the most supportive husband ever, and mother of two adult daughters, one who refuses to leave her home and the other who refuses to tell her where she lives. Of most significance, she is MammyGrams to the sweetest six-year-old, Hadley.

Sheryll worked several years in the fundraising community of Worcester County, writing grants for non-profit organizations. She began writing for her own pleasure after surviving brain surgery and breast cancer. Happily, for her fanbase of family and friends-—she is not dead.

If you have enjoyed reading my book, I would very much appreciate you taking a few minutes to write a review and post that review on amazon.com and goodreads.com.

The opinion of readers can help prospective readers make a purchasing decision.

To learn more, please visit my website, www.pullingthreadsnovella.com subscribe to my blog for updates on future projects.

I would absolutely love to hear from my readers, you can email me at,

pullingthreadsnovella@gmail.com

www.ingramcontent.com/pod-product-compliance
Lightning Source LLC
Chambersburg PA
CBHW070825180626
46818CB00001B/395